THE LIMEH
HAPPENING

By

M E Dormer

RB
Rossendale Books

Published by KDP
A division of Amazon

Published in paperback 2020
Category: Fiction
Copyright M E Dormer © 2020
ISBN : 9798555425560

Original artwork by Sneha Hollis

For David

Chapter 1

One cold grey morning in November a group of Police recruits were sitting in the canteen at Limehouse Police Station. It was a typical Victorian sandstone and red brick building which had seen better days. Although now looking shabby in comparison to the glistening skyscrapers of Canary Wharf, it still commanded a presence in the area. To some a re-assuring sight, to others a place of dread.

The building was given little consideration by the student officers present. Their mood was one of quiet nervousness as today was the day that they would receive the results of the previous week's physical tests. This was the final hurdle, one of many they had encountered during the past twenty weeks, if successful they would take the final written exam. By tomorrow they would know whether, after all those weeks of hard work, their dreams of a Police career were about to come true. They had been attached to Limehouse for the last week of the course to get a sense of what it was really like working in a Police Station environment.

There were fifteen students in total and they came from a variety of backgrounds. Sitting amongst them in the canteen there were also experienced officers, some were offering encouragement, others were adding to their anxiety.

Melanie Bates was sitting at one of the long white melamine tables with a group of recruits. She was an experienced officer, aged around 25, 5'10" with short brown hair, petite and slim. She spoke with an upper-class accent and did not fit the stereotypical Police Officer profile. Melanie's father was a former officer in The British Army, he retired on a full-service pension and now owned his own security company providing services to international organisations. Her mother was a director of a large charity, she often socialised in elite circles, mingling with the great and good. Due to her father's career Melanie had spent most of her life travelling around the world, living for both long and short periods in different countries, and attending different schools. She loved the Army life and thanks to her father's role, combined with families' protection issues she had been trained in both self-defence and the use of firearms. Melanie could handle herself in a fight and gained respect from her colleagues by getting involved when the situation required. Once her father retired from the Army as she wanted to settle down in England it seemed a natural progression for her to become a Police officer.

"So how are you all feeling? Today's the day!" asked Melanie quizzically.

"I think we all did ok in the physical. It's just today's written exam that worries me," replied Carla.

Carla was twenty-five years old, a very attractive girl of mixed heritage. She had a light brown faultless complexion, shoulder length slightly curly brown, hair and piercing green eyes. She did not exploit her looks to make her journey into the force any easier, she had worked and studied very hard to get there, she was not prepared to give anyone a reason to claim that she only got there because of her stunning looks.

"But Carla you've worked so hard, this should be a doddle for you." said Melanie smiling reassuringly.

"I know Mel, just pre-exam nerves I guess," replied Carla with an expression of concern on her face.

"You will all be fine, don't worry. I will catch up with you later. Good luck."

The tension in the room increased when at 8:45am Sergeant Jimmy Jones, the officer in charge of training entered the canteen. He was in his late forties with a grey beard yet kind eyes. His entire demeanour exuded experience mixed with care and consideration. He smiled at the students and said. "You can all make your way downstairs now. They are ready for you."

The students entered Training Room 2, quietly taking their seats, whilst they nervously awaited instructions. On each desk was a computer screen which was already switched on. A large display read 'Click here to begin', with a dialogue box containing the word OK.

Sergeant Jones read out the usual Health and Safety information followed by a briefing on the exam itself.

"When you start you will be presented with twenty questions. Some will be multiple choice, and some will be free text. You have ninety minutes to complete them. If you cannot answer anything please skip the question and move on, there will be an opportunity to return at the end if time allows. Does anybody have any questions? No. Then you may begin."

Chapter 2

At 2.00 pm the shift changeover took place as usual. The officers who had started work at 6.00 am wearily returned their vehicles and completed their day's reports before setting off home in the dull afternoon sun. Following the briefing and having received their postings for the day, the late turn officers started out on their assigned duties.

Monica Lane, an officer with eight years' service, unrivalled experience and an advanced driver was assigned to drive H45, one of the patrol cars. In the passenger seat, and operator for the day was PC Joe Simmonds. She headed out to the back yard of the station where the marked car was parked. After waiting in the driver's seat for a few minutes she called over the radio.

"162 receiving, 135."

After receiving no reply, she repeated the message but a little louder.

"162 receiving, 135!"

"Go ahead."

"I'm waiting to go out."

"On my way, will be two minutes."

Moments later PC Simmonds came rushing out of the building and jumped into the passenger seat.

"Sorry was on the loo," he said looking both flushed and embarrassed.

"Throwing up more like, you look terrible and you smell like a brewery. What time did you get in last night?"

"4 am. I'm never doing that again, only got about 6 hours sleep," he replied wearily.

"4 am? Knowing it was a school night. Hope you feel like you look. You're just lucky that Sargey did the briefing and not the Guvnor."

"What do you mean? He gave me a right bollocking."

"That's what I said, lucky. The Guvor would have done you."

The two of them patrolled their designated beats, Monica was about to comment on how quiet it was when suddenly the radio crackled into life.

"All units, all units. Reports of a large group of males fighting outside Heels Bar in Narrow Street. Any units available? Over."

"We'll take that," said Monica.

"Hotel from Hotel 45, show us assigned."

"Hotel 45 received."

Heels Bar was a very selective members club on the South side of Narrow Street, backing on to the River Thames. Unless you knew of its existence you could easily walk straight past without noticing it. The front resembled a large residential property with an inconspicuous dark green solid front door. The only clues that it was a club were the discreet brass plaque on the wall by the door, and the rather large, smartly dressed doorman standing outside. As it was a members' only club with an expensive annual membership fee it was rare that the Police were ever called to attend. As Monica and Joe arrived it appeared that security had the situation in hand. The large group of males fighting was in fact two young men. The first appeared to be very drunk, he was struggling with the other man, who appeared to be dressed in some sort of dark security uniform, and the doorman. On seeing the Police arrive both men released the drunken male's arms and slightly distanced themselves from him.

The situation appeared to have calmed down and the doorman was ushering the male away as Monica and Joe arrived. They looked at one another, relieved that there would be no need to get involved when suddenly from nowhere the drunk male threw a punch intending to strike the doorman. Unfortunately for him he caught Joe on the jaw.

"Oi!" shouted Joe as he recoiled.

"That's it, you're nicked for assaulting a Police Officer," shouted Monica as she grabbed the man's arm and twisted it behind his back. She handcuffed him and cautioned him before turning to Joe.

"You okay?"

"Yeah it's nothing," replied Joe, rubbing his jaw, and opening and closing his mouth awkwardly.

Once the male was handcuffed and the situation had calmed down Monica looked around for the man in the security uniform. He had disappeared during the melee. The doorman bade them good evening and retreated into the club. Monica, Joe and their detainee remained in the street for several minutes until the Police van arrived to take him back to the station. Monica pressed the doorbell in an effort to establish what had occurred prior to their arrival. The same doorman that had been present at the scuffle answered the door. He told her that the two men had arrived together a little earlier and were trying to gain admission. As he explained that it was a members' club, and that they were not members, the drunken man suddenly became aggressive. Monica asked the doorman if he knew either of them, but the doorman said he had never seen them before. On realising that this incident had run its course Monica got back into her car and drove back to the station behind the van. On arrival at Limehouse Police Station, which was only a short drive away she took charge of her prisoner, who by now was barely awake, and led him into the custody suite.

"One to book in Sarge," said Monica, a line that she had repeated many times before. "Assault on a Police Officer."

The Custody Sergeant, Alan Hall, looked the man up and down, assessing his demeanour in his own mind. He then attempted to obtain the prisoner's details.

"What is your full name please," asked Sergeant Hall.

Drowsily the prisoner looked up and slurring his words replied. "Esther. You need to call Esther."

Sergeant Hall made the decision that he was far too drunk to continue and that it would be best if he slept it off in a cell. All his personal details could be obtained, and his full rights and entitlements given the following morning prior to him being interviewed. Although he was Monica's prisoner, by law the searching officer had to be of the same sex. "Unusual pendant," said Joe as he unfastened the man's necklace and handed it to the Custody Officer.

The Sergeant examined it. It was a fine silver chain with strong links, attached to it was a silver clasp holding a small round stone embellished with strange carved symbols.

"Looks cheap to me," said Sergeant Hall as he sealed it in a property bag, along with the other items that Joe had taken, which he placed in a locked cupboard.

Once this procedure was complete Monica took the prisoner to a cell, she gave him a standard issue blue woollen blanket and placed him on the bench. As he was in such a drunken state, he did not notice that his belt, laces, and all of his possessions had been taken from him. The driving licence in his wallet confirmed his name, Daniel Krowicz, date of birth of 27/03/98 with a Central London address. A business card showed

12

that he worked for an organisation calling itself International Environmental Services.

Monica logged onto one of the station computers in order to complete a name check on Daniel and begin the tedious task of completing all the necessary paperwork. She was convinced that the number of forms to be completed increased every month. The result of the name check revealed no previous convictions however it did display an unusual marker.

If brought to the attention of Police or if detained contact UK International Environmental Services (IES) on internal number 1800.

"Hey Sarge. This bloke's name check came back with an alert marker. It says we need to contact International Environmental Services, whoever they are, with a phone number. I wonder what they want with him?"

"Leave me the printout, I will give them a call shortly," replied Sergeant Hall. Monica then left the charge room and continued completing her paperwork ready for a handover so that an early turn officer could deal with Daniel tomorrow morning.

After around an hour and a half in his cell Daniel started banging loudly on the door. Although he was still drunk and slurring his words he was shouting "My chain! Where is my chain? Give me my chain!"

"It's safe, we have just locked it away until you sober up. You will get it back when you leave tomorrow," replied Sergeant Hall calmly as he slid open the locked viewing hatch. He had dealt with noisy drunks for many years and this one appeared no different to the rest.

"No! I need it now! Give it to me now!" Daniel shouted; he was clearly agitated.

"I told you, you will get it back tomorrow when you leave. Just lie down and sleep it off," Sergeant Hall saw that Daniel was swaying and unsteady on his feet. Obviously still drunk, he thought to himself.

Daniel fell to his knees and looked up at the Sergeant.

"Please just give it to me now. Please!" Daniel begged, but his speech was still slurred.

"Go to sleep Daniel," said the Sergeant as he closed the hatch.

"Call Esther. Call Esther!" demanded Daniel. "Why am I here?" He had a vague recollection of speaking with a man at a bar. Why did he feel so strange? It was almost like being drunk. But I did not have anything to drink, he thought to himself. He then felt a warm feeling all over his body. Oh no, he thought to himself. It has started.

Sergeant Hall walked back to his desk ignoring the noise from Daniel's cell. Remembering the marker that Monica mentioned, he picked up the phone and dialled 1800. A recorded message asked that he leave his details and reason for the call and someone would get straight back to him. He left a message giving Daniel's details and the station where he was being held, placed the telephone back on the receiver and went back to his own never-ending paperwork.

Chapter 3

After completing the exam Carla spent the rest of her shift working in the station front office. The waiting area had been full all day, it mostly comprised people wanting to sign the bail book or produce driving documents. She was grateful to be so busy as it distracted her from thinking about how she might have fared in the exam. She finished duty for the day at 6.00 pm and made her way to the locker room to get changed. She was trying her best to put the exam to the back of her mind and to distract herself she wondered how her grandma was, and what she was going to make her for dinner that evening. Maybe as a treat she would buy an Indian takeaway on the way home, but then on reflection remembering that money was tight she thought it was probably best just to cook. A sad feeling swept over her as she thought about how her grandma's health had deteriorated since the death of her brother. Carla knew that her gran would never get over his death, her heart had been broken and although Carla loved her very much there was nothing that she could do to take away her pain. To hell with it, she thought, I will get a nice takeaway on the credit card. She knew that her grandma liked Indian food.

Melanie also finished her shift at 6.00 pm and walked into the locker room.

"How was your day?" asked Melanie as she rolled her eyes.

"Busy! You don't get a chance to blow your nose in there," replied Carla wearily.

"I know. I hate being posted in there. The queue is relentless, and the punters are painful. It is so much better out on the streets; at least you can manage your own time to some extent. You fancy going for a drink?"

"No ta, I was just going to go home. I'm shattered, plus I live with my gran and I was going to treat her to an Indian takeaway this evening," replied Carla with a worried look on her face.

"What's up?" asked Melanie thinking it had something to do with the exam.

Carla did not reply, she just shrugged her shoulders.

"Come on. You're coming for a drink with me. That's an order," said Melanie authoritatively, whilst smiling in encouragement.

"Ok, but I can't stay long as my gran worries if I am late, plus I want to get the Indian." Carla replied.

They both showered, changed and made their way to the rear exit of the station. They walked out of the building into a dark evening with no moon and stormy rain clouds. There was a slight drizzle in the air which made the pavements shine, reflecting the streetlights.

The Star was an imposing Victorian pub, a five-minute walk from the Police Station. Inside it was traditional and cosy with oak flooring and random non-matching wooden furniture. The bar ran most of the length of the room on the right; the back wall was entirely adorned with ornate mirrors. There were more benches, chairs and tables on the left. In the far corner was a pool table. It was the local drinking hole for most officers at the station and many old pictures with Police themes hung on the walls. There were several other customers, mostly officers, already chatting in groups, some recognised Melanie and acknowledged her as she entered. At the far end of the room were cubicle seating areas, partitioned by shoulder height heavy green curtains which

16

afforded some privacy. Carla and Melanie sat in one of these booths.

"What can I get you?" asked Melanie as she got up and walked towards the bar.

"I'll have a gin and tonic please, I don't care which brands." replied Carla.

Melanie returned with the drinks and sat down opposite Carla. They said cheers, clicked their glasses and took a sip of their drinks.

"Did you hear about Joe Simmonds today?" asked Melanie.

"No. What happened?"

"He got a smack in the mouth from some drunk they nicked."

"Is he ok?"

"He's fine. It was his own fault to be honest. He was so hung over from last night that he couldn't even avoid a drunk's punch. They nicked the bloke, he's in a cell now sleeping it off."

"Mel. Can I ask you something?" said Carla sheepishly.

"Of course, anything?" replied Melanie.

"In training school, we were given a form asking us where we wanted to be posted. I requested Limehouse, but I have heard that we are all being sent to Hackney. I really do not want to go there."

"Well, they post recruits to stations that are short of officers. Hackney is okay, I have worked there. It's remarkably busy and you will learn a lot," replied Melanie. There was reassurance in her intonation.

"It's not that, I just know someone who already works there, and I can't work with him. I didn't mention it before because I never thought they would also post me there too."

"What's the problem Carla?"

Before Carla could reply two men approached their table.

17

"Oh Carla, may I introduce DI Matt Burns and DS Simon Carter," said Melanie as she looked in their direction.

Carla looked at the duo wondering to herself what they wanted.

Matt appeared around thirty years old, he was over 6' with a slim build, wearing a tight shirt, he was obviously fit and in good shape. He had brushed back black hair slightly greying to the sides, blue eyes, slight stubble and a tanned complexion.

Simon looked very much younger, in his mid-twenties, slim, cropped hair, blue eyes and an engaging *'je ne sais quoi'* about him. He was wearing a stylish grey suit with a matching purple shirt and narrow tie.

"Good to meet you Carla," said Matt. "This is Simon my Detective Sergeant, secretary, driver, and general dogsbody." He looked at Simon and smiled.

Simon smiled back as he said, "Lovely to meet you ladies," as he shook hands with them both.

"Sorry Sir, I don't think I've seen you about," replied Carla politely.

"Carla drop the Sir, you're not on duty. Matt please."

"Matt runs the VSO, Victim Support Office. In theory they are attached to Limehouse and have an office here, but their main office is at an offsite covert location," explained Melanie.

"May we join you?" asked Matt.

"Yes of course. Can I get you anything to drink?" replied Melanie.

"No thanks, I'm the on-call DI tonight. We just came in from the station to have a word with someone and saw you two sitting here, Simon do you fancy anything?" replied Matt.

"I will have a vodka and orange with no vodka please, I am the guvnor's driver this evening," replied Simon. Melanie walked over to the bar and soon returned with the drink.

18

"So, Carla, how is it going? I've heard some particularly good things about you," asked Matt with a smile.

"She's stressing out about today's exam," said Melanie before Carla could reply.

"Just the usual exam nerves really. But I love it here in Limehouse I've really enjoyed myself and learned so much," replied Carla, slightly embarrassed by Melanie's earlier comment.

"Well I take it you've heard that this intake is to be posted to Hackney?" said Matt.

"Yes, I have. If that's where they need me then that is where I will go," replied Carla trying to hide her disappointment.

Matt could tell that the idea of going to Hackney did not exactly enthuse her. Good, he thought to himself, she may take me up on my offer.

"Carla. Off the record I have some good news. You two keep this to yourselves but I have been speaking with Sergeant Jones this afternoon about another matter and I found out that you passed the exam. Well done." said Matt.

Carla was overcome with relief. After all those weeks of hard work and worry she had finally done it. The smile on her face showed that she could hardly contain herself. Melanie's earlier conversation slipped from her mind and all that she could do was thank Matt repeatedly. Suddenly she realised that this was a very odd scenario. Why would a Detective Inspector whom she had never met before be giving her the exam results now, in a pub?

"Carla, I know that this intake is being posted to Hackney, but I would like you to stay here. I would like you to be part of my VSO team. I have a position for a trainee working with certain groups and I think you would be ideal. What do you think?"

"But Sir, I have only just started, surely I need to be out on the streets gaining experience. That is why I joined." replied

Carla, hardly believing that she was questioning a Detective Inspector.

"Trust me, lots of officers would like to be on our team, but we look for that potential that you can't quite verbalise," said Simon in his broad Chorley accent.

"Carla you will be out gaining experience, don't worry. In fact, most of the time that is exactly what you will be doing. However sometimes I may need your help. I think you have the type of qualities that we look for in VSO." he explained reassuringly.

"I don't understand Sir. What qualities?"

"Let's discuss it in some more detail tomorrow. Just think it over. Oh, and don't forget to look surprised when they give you your results."

"We will speak soon." The two officers got up to leave, as they did so Simon gave Mel and Carla a cheeky wink and clicked his tongue in his cheek as he said, "Take care."

Both girls looked at one another and smiled. "Simon is nice in a sweet, amusing way," said Mel. "He may look young, but he is as bright as a button. He has an interesting background. Spent most of his career in uniform chasing street rats. He has cracked paedophile rings, rescued unconscious people from burning buildings, managed dangerous informants and that is just a snapshot, terrible driver though. Always crashing Police cars and blaming faulty clutches or brakes. He was very highly thought of and got away with it all using his charm. Subsequently moved to the CID and chosen as Matt's right hand man. Once you get to know him, he has some fascinating stories."

"Single? I didn't notice a wedding ring," asked Carla with an expression of incredulity.

"Not sure, he lives in a flat in the West End, always chatting to the girls. I don't think he has time at the minute. He is always at work."

"Okay, Hackney problem solved. Well done Carla." Melanie smiled to herself. She wondered what Carla's problem with Hackney was. She was going to ask her, but on another day.

"I know. But why me? I mean, I've only just started. Aren't some people going to be put out by this?"

"Who cares what people think? It is Matt's decision and he is a good bloke. You fancy another drink?"

"Thanks Mel but I really should get going. As I said, I am going to get my gran a takeaway and then have an early night."

They both got up to leave and headed for the door. As they did so, they acknowledged colleagues who were still drinking. Outside the evening was still damp with drizzle and there was a cold breeze. The streetlights glowed orange in the misty sky. Carla crossed the road to catch the number 15 bus from outside the church, a short walk from The Star. It was a main road with bright streetlights, so she had no real concerns about walking past the graveyard. Melanie said goodbye and explained that she was going to head back to the station to collect some things that she had forgotten and that she would see her tomorrow. A prawn korma for gran, now, what shall I get? thought Carla as she set off into the cold night.

Chapter 4

Sergeant Hall was sitting at his desk finishing a cup of tea. It had been a quiet shift and he had not booked in any prisoners since the drunken assailant that Monica had arrested. Looking at the clock on the wall he realised that the prisoner welfare checks were due. His jailer had gone the toilet, so he decided to do the checks himself. He was about to get up from his chair when Monica walked in.

"Hello Sarge, here is the rest of the paperwork for Daniel. How is he?"

"Very noisy earlier. I told him to sleep it off and he's been quiet ever since," replied Sergeant Hall in his soft Scottish lilt.

"I was just going to check on him now," he said as he began to get up from his chair.

"It's ok, I can do your checks for you, finish your cuppa," said Monica as she walked towards the cell passage.

At each cell door she opened the clear Perspex section of the viewing hatch, checked inside then fully closed the hatch again and moved on. Most of the prisoners were sleeping; one was just sitting on the bench, staring into space. When she arrived at Daniel's cell, she opened the Perspex section but saw through the plastic that the interior was in total darkness. She moved her face closer, trying to make out any shapes, but it was too dark. She turned her head towards the charge room and shouted to Sergeant Hall.

"Sarge! There's no light in Daniels cell. Can you come down here please?"

At that moment, unknown to Monica, Sergeant Hall was on the phone so he could not reply immediately. As Monica's face was turned towards the charge room, she was unaware of what was happening in the cell in front of her. Two red glowing eyes appeared by the far interior wall and slowly moved closer to the hatch. Monica, still waiting for the Sergeant to reply suddenly felt something was wrong, maybe peripheral vision alerted her, but the eyes, now only inches from her face, were glaring at her. She slowly turned her head towards the hatch and came face to face with the horror of what she saw. The hairs on the back of her neck stood up and she was momentarily frozen with fear. The eyes began to narrow, and she heard a deep throaty growl that filled her with primeval terror. She slammed the hatch shut and jumped back, away from the door. Sergeant Hall was now on his way towards the cell passage after hearing Monica scream.

"What the hell was that! Sarge quick!" shouted Monica as she began to run back towards the charge room.

She ran into Sergeant Hall at the end of the corridor, practically knocking him over, her face was white with fear.

"What's wrong?"

"In Daniel's cell, there's something strange in there. God knows what it is, but it has big red eyes and was growling at me," replied Monica, as she slowly began to calm down.

"Big red eyes? Growling?"

"Sarge, I'm not joking, there is something weird in there," insisted Monica.

"It's just the drunk looking at you," he replied, as he walked towards Daniel's cell.

Sergeant Hall slowly opened the Perspex section of the viewing hatch at arm's length, just in case, he thought to himself. Monica stood at a distance watching as he peered inside. It was so dark that he could not make anything out, so he moved his head closer to the hatch.

"Light must have blown. I can't see a thing."

"Don't get too close Sarge. I'm telling you there's something strange in there."

Sergeant Hall turned towards Monica, rolled his eyes and gave her a dismissive look. His face was now right up to the door as he turned back towards the Perspex staring into the darkness. After a minute or so, when his eyes failed to adjust to the darkness, he re-assured himself that Monica must be mistaken, there was nothing going on other than a blown light bulb. She's imagining things. Again he called out to Daniel through the hatch. Still there was no reply. He closed it and reached for his cell door keys.

"What are you doing? You're not going to open that door please?" shouted Monica.

"Stop messing about and get over here. All you saw was a drunken Daniel. I'm going to go in and check that he's okay. We need to move him to a cell with a light."

He placed the key into the lock, and it turned with a click. Cautiously, he began to open the door, aware that he had not actually seen Daniel yet. He was imagining what Monica said she had seen. Monica, ignoring the Sergeant's requests to assist him, moved further back down the corridor.

"Be careful Sarge," she said as she edged further back down the cell passage towards the charge room.

Sergeant Hall pulled the door half open and looked towards Monica, shaking his head as she moved further away.

Suddenly, Sergeant Hall felt as if he'd been hit by a train. The cell door swung open with such force that it smashed into his right side, lifting him off the floor and throwing him down the cell passage. As he landed with a thud on his back, he grabbed his right arm instinctively as the pain seared through it. From down the passageway Monica saw the door burst open, and Sergeant Hall fly through the air. Shocked, she stepped backwards; losing balance in her haste she rolled onto the floor. Something big and dark caught her eye as she fell. Something that was moving extremely quickly towards the charge room doors. There was a further loud crash and then silence. Both doors had been smashed open and whatever it was had disappeared into the night.

Monica picked herself up off the floor and hit the alarm bar on the wall as hard as she could. She then ran over to Sergeant Hall concerned that he was badly hurt. Within seconds the charge room was full of officers responding to the alarm.

Sergeant Hall and Monica made their way back down the cell passage and into the charge room. They both stared at the broken doors in disbelief, unable to fully comprehend what had just happened.

"Someone call DI Burns please," said Sergeant Hall, as he collapsed into his chair.

DI Burns and DS Carter arrived in the charge room after dashing the short distance from their office. Sergeant Hall was sitting holding his injured right arm and Monica was standing next to him. Both had obviously been shaken up by something. The charge room back doors were open, the lock smashed, and edges of the doors split; they had been broken open with some force.

A short woman, age around fifty with greying hair was speaking with Sergeant Hall. She was smartly dressed in business attire and appeared to be questioning him whilst taking notes.

Monica, still standing at the end of the cell passage called to DI Burns.

"Sir! You might want to look at this," pointing towards Daniel's cell.

The inside of the cell was in total darkness and the reason was obvious. Above them in the ceiling had been a fitted recessed light with a toughened glass cover. It had been smashed to pieces and lay all over the cell floor.

Ripped and torn clothing was strewn around the cell, a pair of shoes lay in the corner. DI Burns and DS Carter looked at one another, each one wondering what had happened. "What do you reckon guvnor?" asked Simon. "I have no idea Simon, but we will get to the bottom of it. Initial thoughts?"

"Let's allow the dust to settle, have a cup of tea and consider what we have got in a logical way, there must be a rational explanation," replied Simon.

Staring into the cell in disbelief, DI Burns could not imagine how anyone could smash that light cover. It was too high to reach, even by standing on the bench.

Having finished their inspection of the cell DI Burns and DS Carter returned to the charge room and were immediately approached by the woman they had seen when they first arrived.

"You must be DI Burns," she said, extending her hand.

"I am. This is DS Carter. May I ask who you are and what you are doing here?" DI Burns replied abruptly.

"My name is Esther Henderson and I work for IES. Sergeant Hall called me a little while ago to inform me of Daniel's arrest. In fact, I arrived shortly before you. This is my identification, and as you can see it gives me authority to enter these, and in fact any Government building that I choose. Getting straight to the point, I will need help from your officers in locating Daniel, as you seem to have lost him. But first, I believe that you have a chain that you took from him when he was arrested. I would like that now please."

DI Burns examined Esther's identification. It looked official enough and to his surprise the signature giving Esther her authority was The Prime Minister. He had never seen an identification pass like it.

"I am the senior officer here, and I will decide what action we are taking," said DI Burns in an attempt to assert his authority.

She took out her mobile phone and headed towards the broken charge room doors.

"No time for chit chat now DI, please get the necklace and follow me. I have two of my staff out there as we speak looking for Daniel, I will give them a call." Esther left the custody suite as she walked into the back yard.

After instructing the officers in the charge room on what action to take to sort out the mess and collecting the necklace, DI Burns and DS Carter walked into the back yard to see Esther speaking on the phone. As they did so Melanie was walking towards them from the street.

"What is going on here guvnor? I don't like it. Who is the doris?" said Simon in a hushed but serious tone.

"Simon, you are as wise as I am at the moment," he replied, his voice filled with agitation.

"Oh my God! What on earth happened to the doors?" asked Melanie as she looked towards the damage.

At that moment Esther finished her phone call.

"We think he has headed for the graveyard outside the church, my staff are checking from the South side now. We can enter from the North. Where do we need to go?" asked Esther.

"You can enter through the gates from the main road, they never lock them. We need to go out onto the street and turn right, it is a five-minute walk. Exactly why are you interested in Daniel and is he dangerous? I mean, do I call in armed response?" asked DI Burns.

"No! most certainly not. We can handle the situation. Do you have the necklace?" said Esther.

27

Esther took the necklace from DI Burns and headed towards the street.

"I'll call you if I need anything," Esther shouted as she walked away.

"Sir, I don't know what's going on here, but Carla lives in Shadwell and goes home that way. She could be around there now, she catches the 15 bus outside the graveyard," said Melanie, concerned that her friend might be in danger.

"Wait! We're coming with you." DI Burns shouted as he, DS Carter and Melanie ran to catch up with Esther.

Chapter 5

A makeshift tent was secreted in the bushes and trees that grew in the graveyard around the side of the old church. It was made from a tarpaulin tied between the trees to give cover from the elements. Beneath it, an old mattress lay on the ground. Empty beer cans and food packets were strewn around, this was home to Anton and Ratko, two Bulgarians. Their dreams of a new life in England never quite worked out, and copious amounts of cheap beer helped both pass the nights and keep out the cold. The graveyard was filled with old overgrown abandoned gravestones, most at angles, some had even completely fallen over. The people who once cared for them had long since passed away themselves. Nobody remembered the graves' inhabitants, and nobody really cared. Looking out from their camp Ratko thought that he spotted something moving between the gravestones in the distance. Catching glimpses of it lumbering slowly heading towards the church wall he couldn't quite make out its shape. Was it a dog? A big dog if it was. Straining his eyes to make it out, he realised that it had turned and was now looking in their direction. He jumped back with fear as he saw the two glowing red eyes staring straight at him. Reaching out he grabbed his friend and pulled him towards him pointing out into the distance.

"Anton! Look! Out there! There is something out there, some beast," he exclaimed as they retreated into their tent.

Anton stared into the darkness, slowly scanning the extensive graveyard.

"There is nothing there," he said, taking another drink from his can.

"I saw it. It had big red eyes. It was Varcolac," said Ratko with fear in his voice.

Anton felt a chill run down his spine on hearing the name Varcolac and turned to look out into the darkness. Both men stared into the night, neither making a sound.

Eventually, "There is nothing out there. You are drunk," said Anton.

Turning to get further back under the cover of their makeshift shelter both men froze when they heard the crack of a twig and low heavy breathing from the side of their tent nearest to the church.

Meanwhile, unaware of the drama about to unravel in front of her, Carla made her way towards the bus stop, she could see the church gates up ahead and the stop was a few yards beyond that. As she approached the gates, she heard loud voices in what she thought were an Eastern European language. They seemed to be coming in her direction from inside the graveyard. Suddenly, two men ran out from the gates heading towards her, as they did so, one of them dropped something on the floor. Instinctively she stopped, taking her hands out of her pockets prepared to defend herself. But instead of attacking her they just stared at her, fear in their eyes. "Varcolac! Varcolac!" they shouted, before running off into the distance. She approached the gates cautiously and noticed an iron bar on the ground. She took her phone out and started to dial the number for Limehouse control room. As she waited for the call to be answered she could hear something coming from the direction of the church, it sounded like a low whimpering noise. Eventually someone in the control room answered the call and Carla explained the situation. She advised that officers would be on their way shortly and told her to wait until they arrived. In her mind Carla knew that it would probably not be an immediate response, no doubt there would be minimal officers on patrol. Then she heard it again, a soft whimper, someone was hurt. She couldn't just wait around; she had to investigate and see if she could help. Carla gingerly made her way into the graveyard heading towards the church, following the noise.

DI Burns' radio alerted him that a call had been received from an off-duty Police Officer stating that there had been some kind of incident in the graveyard by the North Gate entrance. The radio operator informed him that the station van was on its way, but that that it was travelling from Bethnal Green and would be about ten minutes. DI Burns called the control room.

"Hotel Control from DI Burns can you also show me and DS Carter attending. Over."

"Yes, received sir. You also have the van about ten minutes away, over," came the reply.

"Hotel Control from DI Burns. Which officer called this in?"

"It was Carla Sir."

"Received. DI Burns out."

DI Burns, DS Carter and Melanie caught up with Esther who was still walking purposefully in the direction of the church, which was looming out of the drizzle in the distance. There was hardly any traffic on the road and only a few pedestrians were braving the cold damp weather. The four of them glanced at one another in acknowledgement and continued walking, hurriedly.

Carla entered the graveyard and slowly walked along the path towards the church. The streetlights glow barely reached that far. The dilapidated gravestones and overgrown shrubbery added to the eeriness. She could make out some torn down tarpaulin lying on top of an old mattress, there were beer cans and rubbish on the floor, but no one was around. She squinted as she looked towards the side of the church where she could make out what looked like a smear of blood on the wall. To the left of the steps leading up to the main church entrance were two dark blue wooden doors, which were open, the area around the locks were splintered and broken. She peered inside and saw stone steps leading down into the crypt. Again, she heard the whimpering noise; it was coming from the darkness beyond the foot of the steps. Carla edged slowly down, descending one by one as quietly as she could. She craned her neck looking into the darkness, as her eyes grew accustomed to the dark, she made out the shape of something lying on the flagstone floor. It was an animal, though she could not make out what type, it was lying on all fours facing away from her. Long dark fur covered its body. She noticed that the front pad was cut and bleeding. The animal was shaking as it whimpered in the cold. What was it? It was certainly not a dog, more like an ape she thought. Fear began to take over from adrenaline and she knew that she had to get away before it noticed her. Stepping backwards she slowly walked up the steps. Suddenly she slipped on the damp stone, landing sitting on a step. The animal immediately raised its head and slowly turned to face her. Carla froze with fear as the two red eyes stared at her out of the darkness. She could now see that its face was covered in flame coloured fur. It made a low growl as it lay there motionless. Carla instinctively felt the need to remain still and definitely not make any quick movements. Just as she convinced herself that the animal was about to attack her it slowly lay down its head, there was a look of fear in its eyes. It continued to whimper with a vulnerable frightened expression if that was possible for whatever the animal was. Carla could see a large gash on the top of the animal's head, it was bleeding profusely, it was clearly hurt.

"It's okay. It's okay, I won't hurt you," said Carla in a low soft voice.

Carla slowly moved closer as the animal seemed to realise that she posed no threat. The animal's head was now on the floor and its eyes were barely open as it continued to whimper. Carla slowly reached out her hand and stroked its front paw. There was no reaction from the animal, its eyes were almost closed, and she knew that it was badly hurt. Thinking back to the iron bar that she had seen on the ground outside, she concluded that the two men that she saw must have attacked it. Suddenly she heard voices coming from the graveyard outside. Someone was calling her name, then at the top of the steps she saw DI Burns, DS Carter and Melanie with Esther, whom she did not know. Carla looked back at the animal, wondering whether it would react to the voices outside, but its eyes were now closed, and it did not move. Carla looked up in the direction of the top of the staircase and placed her finger to her lips in a sign to the others to be quiet. She saw Esther whisper something to DI Burns, she then descended the steps towards her.

"Carla I am going to hand you a necklace. Can you please place it onto the animal's back for me? There is no need to fasten it round its neck. Don't worry it will not harm you."

Carla took the necklace and gently placed it above the animal's shoulder so that it lay at the base of its neck. She wondered to herself what this was all about, as it appeared very strange.

"Now Carla, slowly back away and come out of there," said Esther.

Carla had no problem with that request and did as instructed, feeling relieved that the others were there and someone else had taken control, but she also felt sorrow for the poor animal.

"I think it is badly hurt. I saw two men running from the graveyard and one of them dropped an iron bar. I think they attacked it. It has a big gash on its head," said Carla once she got outside.

"What do you mean it's badly hurt, isn't that Daniel down there?" asked DI Burns.

"Daniel? Who's Daniel? No, it's some type of animal, an ape I think," replied Carla, by now totally mystified.

As this conversation was taking place two of Esther's colleagues arrived, they were dressed in black uniforms with green edging to the sleeves and collars and stood a few feet away speaking with Esther in hushed tones. A few seconds later the three of them walked over to DI Burns.

"Well I would like to thank you for all your help, and we will deal with matters from here." said Esther.

"Erm Esther, aren't you forgetting something?" said DI Burns.

"And what's that?" she replied.

"We came here looking for an escaped prisoner called Daniel. Remember?"

"A full report will be with you first thing tomorrow. Thank you for your help but we will take it from here," replied Esther as she walked down the steps towards the crypt followed by her two colleagues.

"I still have a missing prisoner who was initially arrested for assaulting a Police Officer. I don't care whom you work for, but I am not leaving until I get a full explanation of what is going on here." said DI Burns as he stood in the doorway at the top of the steps.

"Nick her guvnor, I don't like her anyway," whispered Simon under his breath. "That is a stone bonker obstructing a Police Officer, I have nicked people for far less."

"Simon, I don't doubt that for one minute," he replied. "We are just going to have to sit this one out. I don't know who they are, but their authority would appear to be higher than ours."

"I already told you DI Burns, you will get your report tomorrow," shouted Esther haughtily from inside the crypt.

DI Burns, DS Carter, Carla and Melanie stood looking at one another in the graveyard; it was still drizzling and damp. They were all trying to make sense of what had just happened. As they stood there the station van pulled up by the gates and the four of them slowly walked over. As they did so they saw that one of Esther's colleagues was walking towards the gate behind them. The four of them reached the van and DI Burns explained to the officers that no assistance was required as the situation had been dealt with. He thought that it was probably best at this stage to give out minimal information. This was in part because he did not actually have any concrete information to give and in part because he knew that it involved senior members of Government and The Civil Service. He instructed the van crew to continue with their allocated patrol. As the Police van pulled away, a dark blue transit van stopped next to Esther's colleague who had been waiting by the side of the road. The driver handed over a large black bag and Esther's colleague took it and walked back into the graveyard and down into the crypt.

"Sir. What is going on here? Who is that woman?" asked Carla, clearly frustrated at having no clue what was happening.

"All I know Carla is that she has very senior Government authority and is telling me nothing. Are you okay, what did you see down there?"

"Yes, Sir I'm fine, a bit shaken, but part of that is because I slipped on a wet step. I went in because I thought someone was hurt but it turned out to be an animal, a strange ape-like animal with red eyes. I must admit that I was scared; I thought it was going to attack me, but it just lay there. Then I noticed that it was badly hurt and bleeding," explained Carla.

"What was it that she gave you down there?" asked Melanie.

"It was a necklace that Daniel was wearing when he was arrested, it was taken from him before he was placed in his cell. I have no idea of its relevance," replied DI Burns.

In the distance meanwhile, Esther and her two colleagues were leaving the graveyard. They were helping a young man with dark hair and a bandage around his forehead. He was wearing a grey tracksuit and had a blanket over his shoulders. They stopped at the van and the young man looked over in their direction as if talking about them. He appeared to be arguing with Esther. Esther briefly looked in the direction of the four officers, then turned to one of her colleagues.

"Aidan get their names to Kevin. Tell him I want to know everything about those four."

Esther and her entourage then climbed into the back of the blue transit van and it drove off into the night heading towards Central London.

"Where on earth did he come from?" asked Melanie.

"I don't know, let's take a proper look at the scene," suggested DS Carter. The four officers walked back into the graveyard, where they descended the steps into the crypt.

"Hair, the floor is covered in hair," observed Melanie.

They stood in silence for a few minutes looking at the floor and then staring at each other. Carla bent down and picked up some lengths.

"This is crazy, this can't be, that guy, he must have been.......?" said Carla, unable to finish the ridiculous sentence.

36

"That animal you saw, it was him; it was Daniel!" replied DI Burns. "No wonder she didn't need to look for him, she already knew where he was. It is vital that none of us say anything about this to anyone, that is an order." The girls nodded in agreement as they hurriedly left and walked back towards the station. "DS Carter will drive you both to your homes."

Parked outside the station was a racing green P6 Rover. "Get in ladies," said Simon. "This is my pride and joy." He drove carefully but progressively through the damp streets. First he dropped off Melanie, then Carla. As Carla walked into her building and up the stairs to the flat, she was still trying to make some sense of what had just happened. Suddenly she realised that she was supposed to bring her gran an Indian takeaway, and in all the excitement she had forgotten. I will just order a delivery she thought to herself as she unlocked the door and let herself in.

"Hi gran it's only me. You fancy Indian tonight?" she shouted as she closed and double locked the door.

Chapter 6

The following day DI Burns was rostered to start work at 10.00 am but he and DS Carter had decided to get in early to review the previous day's incident in the custody suite in the cold light of day. They wanted to speak to Sergeant Hall and establish whether Esther had sent a report as promised. On entering the back yard, they could see that both doors had been repaired, in fact they looked as good as new. It was strange as the maintenance company would normally take some measurements and make a temporary fix; they would then return the next day to complete the repair fully. Unusually these were brand new doors and frames. Maybe we are using a different maintenance company, DI Burns thought to himself. They entered the station and made their way to the charge room. The staff had all changed since yesterday's incident and the Custody Officer was now Sergeant Daniela Bloom. She was a large lady, in her forties with blonde wavy hair. She looked like a favourite aunty however beneath that sweet exterior she was as hard as nails and stood for no nonsense.

"Good Morning Daniela, any news from Alan Hall today? I know the ambulance crew checked him out and he went home early yesterday, just wondering if he called in today," asked DI Burns.

"Good morning Matt," she replied cheerily. She and Matt were old friends having been Sergeants together during a previous posting. "Yes actually, he called earlier. He said he feels fine and his arm is just a little bruised. Strangely, he told me that he has been informed that he has an appointment at that Private

Medical Centre in Three Colt Street. Meanwhile, he has been given two weeks sick leave on full pay, which will not count towards his sick record. I had no idea we have benefits like that."

"We don't," replied DI Burns in a sarcastic tone.

DS Carter inspected the new doors before turning back to Daniela.

"It looks like we have a new maintenance company Dan. That's a pretty good job."

"Nope Simon, it wasn't the usual lot. Some Government supply company came in last night. Took out the broken doors and replaced them with those. They even touched up some of the surrounding paintwork and fitted the new locks and door alarm system. And they fixed the cell light. They had all the paperwork and The Commissioner signed it off, no less. Weird don't you think?"

"Yes, very weird," replied Simon. Everything about yesterday was weird, he thought to himself. He was convinced that this was all Esther's doing. He looked through the custody log checking on the status of Daniel's record. As he suspected, the entry was marked as cancelled and all property had been collected and signed for. It was as if Daniel had never been there.

"Looking for something specific Simon?" asked Daniela.

"No. No, its fine," he replied with a grin on his face.

"Okay guvnor, come on let's go to the office and have a cuppa. We need to think carefully about where we are going with this one if anywhere." They headed towards the office, wondering what other surprises Esther had in store. They didn't have long to wait.

***

Carla woke early that morning, despite having not managed to get much sleep. She had spent most of the night thinking about the events in the graveyard, trying to make sense of it all. After showering and dressing for work she went about her usual routine of preparing breakfast for her gran. As usual, gran was already up and watching television in the living room. Carla said her usual good morning, placed two slices of toast into the toaster and flicked on the kettle. After all these years she knew that was all her grandma ever wanted, just two slices of toast and a cup of tea. She stood in the kitchen as her gran watched television. In the corner of her eye she caught sight of the two charcoal sketches hanging on the wall. Her older brother Stephen loved to paint and draw. Betty, her gran, had bought him a pad and some coloured pencils for his ninth birthday. He was thrilled with his present, and Betty kept all his paintings. She remembered when her brother made her sit on the sofa so that he could sketch her. A feeling of guilt washed over her as she recalled to herself how awkward she was when he tried to get her to sit still. "CJ! Stop fidgeting," he would shout. How she wished she could sit still for him now, her brother, her hero.

***

Carla Jasmin Brown was born on the 18th of October 1999. Her mother's name was Christine and her father's Patrick. Her mother gave birth to her brother Stephen four years earlier and they lived in a two bedroomed council flat in Lambeth. Not that Carla could remember any of that. At the age of four her mother took both her and her brother to their grandmother Betty's flat in Shadwell. She then left the two children with just a bag of clothes between them and walked away. Carla had neither seen nor heard from either of her parents since that day and had no desire to do so. Her grandmother had borne witness to the squalor of the flat in Lambeth. She had seen the bruises that appeared on Stephen as their parents continued a downward spiral into drug abuse. Betty eventually applied for custody of the children. At the court hearing neither of Carla's parents contested the application and custody was granted. Betty was aged fifty-four when she took the children in. Things were not easy, and money was always tight, but they were fed, clothed, taken to school and loved. Betty had brought them up well and encouraged them to study so that they could make something of their lives. As with all children there were occasions when Carla misbehaved. On those occasions Stephen would call her CJ. Betty would say "Carla Jasmin Brown get here now child." Carla had very fond memories of the time when all three of them lived together.

Then at around 8.00 pm on the 3rd of August 2012 something happened that would change all of their lives forever. Stephen was walking along Commercial Street in Aldgate on his way home from an art class. It was a journey that he had often made and took around twenty minutes. As he made his way through the balmy evening sunshine, he noticed a young girl visibly upset as she was being harassed by a group of young men. Stephen had stopped to ask if she was okay and asked them to leave her alone. The group became aggressive and one of them pulled out a kitchen knife and stabbed Stephen in the stomach. Stephen fell to the ground and the assailant's accomplice then kicked him in the head. The attackers ran off and the girl ran screaming into a nearby shop, staff called the Police and Ambulance. Stephen died in hospital three days later with Betty and Carla by his bedside. The head injury had been so severe that he never regained consciousness.

Since that day Betty's health had gone downhill, something in both her and Carla died with Stephen, and a pain was born that would never go away. Carla had thought of what a great help their Family Liaison Officer, PC Angela Smith had been. She visited them almost every day and kept them up to date with the progress of the investigation. She even attended Stephen's funeral. She was there all the way through the pain of the trial and to this day still sends a Christmas card. Carla had decided that she wanted to be a Police Officer. She wanted to be like Angela, she wanted to do what she could so that no other family would go through the pain that she and Betty went through every day of their life. Stephen would have been proud of her decision.

Carla stayed on at school into the sixth form, completing her A levels. After leaving she applied for and was accepted for the role of Police Community Support Officer. She had wanted to experience what the job entailed before committing to a full-time career in the Police. She spent the next year and a half working at Stoke Newington Police Station and that is where she met PC Adrian Denham. She was out with colleagues one evening when she was introduced to him. Adrian was a dog handler and was based at Hackney Police Station. He was charming, funny and was immensely popular with his colleagues. Carla had dated before but nothing serious, certainly not enough to take them home to meet Betty. Adrian was different. Carla felt close to him and he showered her with attention. He wanted to see her every evening when they were both off duty and he called her all the time. Carla had been seeing Adrian for about three months when she decided to take him to her home. Betty had welcomed him and was polite, although Carla could tell that she did not really take to him. Maybe Betty thought that having lost Stephen, she would lose Carla as well. One evening Carla had agreed to meet Adrian after her late shift but subsequently decided that she was too tired. She went home and spent the evening with Betty. Carla was dozing on the sofa when the doorbell rang at about midnight. Betty answered the door and saw that it was Adrian; he was asking if Carla was home. Betty explained that Carla was sleeping and that she did not want to disturb her as she was tired, but Adrian would not leave. He pushed his way past Betty into the flat, as he did so he caused her to fall to the floor injuring her hip.

Carla heard the noise, woke up and saw Adrian walking into the living room. He accused her of seeing someone else and told her that she ought to move into his flat with him. Carla ran over to Betty who was lying on the floor in the hallway, and after seeing what he had done screamed at him to get out. He refused to leave and grabbed Carla by the hand as he attempted to drag her out of the flat. Carla pulled back with all her strength as she resisted him. Adrian then slapped Carla across the face and pulled at her again. Carla was by now filled with rage as she clenched her fist and smashed it into his nose, which spread across his face and immediately started to bleed. Screaming at the top of her voice for him to get out, he finally left. As he did so he told her not to even think about reporting this because if he lost his job his friends would make sure that her life in the Police would be hell.

Betty went to hospital for her hip to be examined. The fall had stretched a tendon causing a permanent limp, something that Carla would never forgive herself for. Carla was now full of hatred towards Adrian, not only for what he had done to Betty, but also for his threats towards her. How dare he hurt Betty? She decided that she was going to make him pay no matter what happened to her at work. Betty had heard what he had said to Carla and knew what problems he could cause for her. She knew that life was going to be tough enough for Carla without Adrian making it even tougher. Betty begged Carla not to report him; she did not want her little girl having to deal with the victimisation that would surely follow. Carla knew that if she did report the incident Adrian would lose his job. She also knew that he was popular amongst his peers, and what he had said was very possible. There was a good chance that his friends would make her life an absolute misery, so she decided not to report it. It was with great reluctance that she took Betty's advice but vowed to herself that she would never see him again.

Carla gave Betty her tea and toast and said goodbye. She left the flat and headed through Watney Street Market towards the number 15 bus stop on the main road, wondering what the day was going to bring. Did all that really happen yesterday evening? Maybe I will get off the bus and walk past the church and look in the graveyard, she thought to herself.

Chapter 7

"Coffee Guvnor"? said Simon as he switched on the percolator. "Yes, please Simon," replied DI Burns as he logged onto his computer to check his emails. To his surprise the promised report from Esther was not there. Very strange he thought, as she had been so efficient at sorting everything else out. Almost immediately a meeting invitation message appeared on the screen.

You are required to attend the conference room on the third floor at 9:30 am. Please ensure that you also bring Simon Carter, Melanie Bates and Carla Brown.

DI Burns sipped on his coffee. "This is odd Simon, look at this," he said as he showed Simon the invitation. He logged his computer off and they made their way to the canteen, where Carla and Melanie were waiting. He wondered why he had doubted Esther's promise to have the report ready, but he was surprised that she was here to present it in person. The two of them walked over to where Carla and Melanie were already speaking quietly to one another, DI Burns led the way. There could be no doubt. It was obvious that the two of them were talking about the events of yesterday.

"We have been summonsed."

"Summonsed? By whom?"

"Esther. She wants to see us now on the third floor. Ready? Let me do all the talking."

"Maybe we will finally find out what this is all about. I didn't sleep a wink last night and locked all my windows and doors. To think that something like that could be out there somewhere doesn't bear thinking about," said Melanie indignantly.

They got up from the table, and the four of them made their way to the third floor eager to hear what Esther had to say.

"Sir. I went into the graveyard on my way here this morning. The door has been repaired and the mattress and tent and even the rubbish has all gone," said Carla.

"Why am I not surprised? Just wait until you see the custody suite doors." replied DI Burns.

The four of them entered the conference room. Esther was sitting at the end of a long wooden table surrounded by chairs. She was wearing a dark pin striped business suit. In front of her on the table was an open briefcase. She watched them intently as they entered, then averted her eyes to the contents of the case.

"Good morning. Please be seated," said Esther without looking up.

They all took seats, two of them to the left, and two of them to the right of Esther. Sitting in silence DI Burns wondered what cover story Esther had come up with to explain the events of the previous night. He gave DS Carter a look as if to say, "What old flannel are we about to hear?" Simon returned the look discreetly. The two men knew exactly how each other ticked without needing to say a word. Esther took a pair of half-moon spectacles from here breast pocket and put them on, balancing them on the end of her nose. She then took two buff card folders from her briefcase and placed them on the desk and closed the briefcase.

Opening one of the folders Esther examined the contents, flicking through the pages without raising her vision. After a few moments she looked up from the folder, over the top of her glasses and stared at DI Burns.

46

"Thank you for meeting me this morning officers. I have prepared two files here and before submitting them I would just like to clarify that all the facts are correct. One will be submitted to the Independent Police Complaints Commission and the other to the Crown Prosecution Service."

"What?" said DI Burns, in a raised voice, with an air of disbelief.

"Please! Do not interrupt me. DI Burns, I understand that following Daniel's arrest he was placed in a cell without being medically examined despite showing signs that he was unwell. Is that true?"

"I was not present at the time that Daniel was booked in." replied DI Burns.

"I see. Subsequent to Daniel having been placed in a cell, despite becoming anxious he was ignored and was still not offered medical help. Is that correct?" asked Esther.

"Daniel was drunk, he had assaulted a Police officer, and there was nothing about him to suggest that he was any different to any other belligerent drunk." DI Burns replied angrily.

"You may be interested to know that when examined by a medical professional no alcohol was found in Daniel's system. Did you call IES immediately after seeing the alert message shown when his name was checked?" demanded Esther.

"As I said, I was not there but my Custody Officer, Sergeant Hall did as soon as it became practical, he has responsibility for the welfare of the prisoners. As you will be aware there were more prisoners than just Daniel to look after. At my rank as you know, I cannot order the Custody Officer to take any particular course of action," DI Burns replied, now worried about where this was going.

"So, the Custody Sergeant didn't call IES immediately? When he was finally checked, your officers saw that due to his distressed state, he had removed all his clothing. They then simply allowed him to walk out of the custody suite in his confused and naked state into a cold dark wet street. Is that correct?" Esther asked staring directly at DI Burns.

"No, that is not what happened, and you know it," replied DI Burns in an agitated voice.

"Exactly where were you when this vulnerable young man was being detained in this manner?" asked Esther with an enquiring look, again peering over the top of her glasses.

"I was discussing an operational matter with a colleague." DI Burns replied, now realising exactly where the questioning was leading.

"I did not ask what you were doing. I asked, exactly, where were you? Were you the 'On call' Detective Inspector for yesterday evening when all this was happening?" Esther said leaning towards DI Burns.

"I was in The Star." DI Burns replied angry.

"The Star being the local public house. Is that correct?" asked Esther, now sitting back in her chair.

"Yes."

"We were engaged on a confidential enquiry, and our duty sheets noted that at the time," interrupted DS Carter. He was clearly irritated at the direction of Esther's questions.

"DS Carter, I do not require any input from you, thank you. You too were in The Star, also on duty. You are facing the same fate as your DI."

"So, to sum up, this vulnerable male, in desperate need of medical attention was placed in a cell. His cries for help were ignored, and then he was allowed to escape from your custody and run naked into the street. When he was finally found we discover that he had been violently assaulted. And while all this was going on in your Police Station, you were both in The Star." Esther closed the file and placed it onto the desk.

DI Burns stared at her in disbelief. He knew that technically she was right. The way that she was slanting the report there was a possibility that they could both be facing discipline, or even end up being fired.

"This is wrong. This is all……" DI Burns tried to explain.

"I haven't finished speaking yet!" shouted Esther in an agitated tone.

Esther then picked up the second file and again without looking up she flicked through the pages. Carla and Melanie could not believe what they had just heard. They expected to be given some explanation of what happened last night but not this. Both wondered who was next to incur Esther's wrath.

"Police Constable Brown. Would you say that one of the most important values of any Police Officer is honesty?"

"Yes, I would." Carla replied cautiously.

"And do you think that any Officer deliberately withholding information regarding a criminal offence that they had committed should remain in their position?"

"No, they probably shouldn't." Carla replied, unsure what Esther was getting at. I have never committed any criminal offence she thought to herself.

Esther went on; "I have here a signed and dated statement from PC Adrian Denham. In it he states that you violently attacked him in a fit of anger causing serious injuries to his face. Although he did not report it at the time because he did not want to get you into trouble he has since learned that you have become a Police Officer. He says that he feels it is now his duty to report this as you may be a risk to the public given your office."

Carla could hardly believe her ears. That scumbag had not only assaulted and threatened her; but had also injured Betty.

"That is not what happened. He not only assaulted me but also threatened me. He also assaulted my grandmother," replied Carla angrily.

"You will have your chance to defend yourself in court," replied Esther with a dismissive air.

Carla could not believe that this was happening to her. She had only just started her career in the Police and now she was not only going to be fired, but probably thrown in prison as well.

Esther then turned to Melanie and asked. "Police Constable Bates. How long have you been a Police Officer?"

"Just over two years." Melanie replied, dreading what she was going to be accused of.

"And if an officer is a witness to another officer's gross neglect of duty should they report this immediately?"

"Yes, to their supervisor."

"And if the officer committing the act of negligence is their supervisor, who then should they report it to?"

"They should report it to an officer of higher rank," she replied, knowing exactly what was coming next.

"Yet when you witnessed a senior officer you knew to be on duty in a pub you failed to report it. Even when you later found out that a vulnerable prisoner had escaped and been assaulted while this officer was in the pub you still failed to report this?"

Melanie said nothing and looked down at the table as she wondered what would happen to her.

Esther unlocked her briefcase, placed both folders inside then locked it again and placed it on the floor.

"These are the files that will be submitted." Esther paused, looking at all four officers in turn.

"Or they would be if I had my way. Fortunately for you, someone else has a different idea. You will be contacted shortly for a meeting. I trust not a word of recent events will be mentioned to anyone. I hope I have made myself clear. Good morning." With that she picked up her briefcase and walked out of the room.

Chapter 8

Esther Henderson reversed her red electric convertible car into her reserved parking space in the company car park. Dressed in a dark blue formal outfit she picked up her briefcase and headed into the IES building passing at least six CCTV cameras on the way. At the main entrance stood a guard dressed in a black military style uniform, a dark green trim to the jacket and a gold badge with Ranger written on it. As Esther placed her right index finger on the reader pad, he did not even acknowledge her presence although Esther knew that anyone attempting to enter the building without authorisation would find themselves unable to gain access. Several specially selected Rangers were armed with Glock 38 pistols. Globally, IES buildings had been targeted by extremist environmental organisations; several staff had even been assaulted. These groups believed that IES was a secret government programme responsible for the dramatic climate changes taking place. If only they knew, she thought to herself. After passing through several more security systems Esther headed straight for the conference room, the day was an important one and everything had to go exactly to plan. The décor of the meeting room was minimalist, in keeping with the general style of the building. Brilliant white walls, white fittings, a grey speckled carpet. At one end were floor to ceiling windows. The walls were adorned with large framed colour photographs of flora and fauna in subtle grey metal frames with a variety of mounts contrasting with the content. In the centre of the room was a circular glass table with a shiny chrome frame surrounded by twelve matching chairs with grey padded cushion seats. Against one wall was a light wooden sideboard with a coffee machine; next to it was a water fountain. Esther took her seat at the table. Four other attendees were already seated and were chatting as Esther sat down. Immediately to her left were Professors Oliver Chambers and Sonia Fielding. To her right were Ranger Aidan Preston and Head Technician Kevin Hart. Esther looked around the table, coughed authoritatively, placed her glasses on the end of her nose, and took her laptop from her briefcase.

"Good morning ladies and gentlemen. As you know, three months from today the international conference will take place at the IES Exhibition Centre. We intend to keep the front of house exhibits up and running and open to the public. As is usual however we are creating a private area to the rear of the Centre for the specimens to be housed whilst they are being transferred. To ensure that everything runs smoothly I will be chairing a weekly meeting every Tuesday at 8.00 am in this meeting room until opening day. I expect a weekly written progress report from each of your departments by close of play on the previous Friday, highlighting any problems or issues that you may foresee. The meeting will last no longer than an hour so please keep the contents relevant. No grandstanding allowed. Professor Chambers, your update please."

"Good morning Esther. Installation of all the cabinets containing the botanical specimens are now complete. We had a little trouble with the South American set up, but Kevin and his team have come up with a method of controlling the constant flow of water that is required. South American, Indian and Japanese field crews have approved them and are arranging transport with the co-operation of our Rangers," replied Professor Chambers, spilling his coffee as he placed his cup on the table.

Esther looked at him as he wiped up the spillage with a handkerchief. So intelligent but so clumsy, she thought to herself.

"Good well-done Oliver. I assume that the alarms are in place for the Japanese specimen?"

"Sorry about the coffee. Yes, Kevin has personally installed them. There is one thing though, the South Americans insist on their Rangers being present at all times, right up until the transfer to Eden 14."

"I'm not surprised considering the specimen. Ranger Preston are you happy with that arrangement?" asked Esther.

"That will be fine, they have been briefed and are aware that they cannot enter Eden 14. We will make all the necessary arrangements with them and take over from there." he replied.

"Professor Fielding your update; please."

"The environmental habitats are complete, and they have been approved by the field crews, however the Americans have concerns and I think that they may pull out. The accident last October has them worried. They lost two Rangers and are concerned about safety. I have been working with their field crews and they are happy that the habitats are suitable so maybe a word from you might allay their fears. In addition to that the Chinese have insisted that their technical teams be present to ensure that the environmental systems are always fully operational. If you and Kevin are happy with those arrangements, I will pass that on," she replied.

"I fully understand their concerns. It was an awful tragedy, but I also realise how vitally important it is for us to have their specimen present. I will speak to Daniel. Kevin are you happy to work with the Chinese?" asked Esther.

"Yes of course, that will be fine, maybe we can steal some of their secrets," replied Kevin, smiling.

"Any other problems at your end?" asked Esther.

"No everything is on schedule. The private area wall goes in tomorrow and the extra CCTV system is being fitted today. The main private area entrance door will be an air lock system with a complete lockdown facility should the control room or Rangers activate it. The specimen docking pods on the riverside have been completed and we are just awaiting arrival timetables."

"And the American docking pod has been thoroughly tested?" asked Esther, raising her eyebrows.

"Yes, with the complete co-operation of their field crews."

"Thank you, Kevin."

"Ranger Preston your update please."

"Private accommodation areas for all our guests has been arranged and is staffed twenty-four hours a day by Rangers. Escorts to and from the Centre will also be arranged. Rangers will staff entrance areas within the complex, both public and private. All access passes will go through Ranger control and most have now been issued. Rangers will be carrying firearms within the private area in case there should be any attempt to gain entry," he replied.

Esther looked around the table with an approving expression on her face.

"Good. We seem to be on track. I do not need to remind you how important it is that we get this right. The specimens will be at the Centre for two days before being transported to Eden 14 so make the most of your time with them. On another note, it has come to my attention that somehow information about the projects has been leaked. Aidan and his team are working on identifying the source. Once it is discovered, the person responsible will be dealt with most severely. You must stay alert and if you suspect anything or anyone report it immediately to Aidan. Thank you for your updates. Are there any questions before we close the meeting?"

"Yes, will the book be there?" asked Professor Fielding.

"Daniel has not yet decided. In my opinion it should not be, and I have advised him of that. As soon as he decides, I will let you know. If that is all then I will see you all tomorrow. Aidan, can you wait behind please?"

Those present collected their possessions and left the room. Esther finished typing her notes and placed her laptop back in her briefcase.

"Have you got any further with your investigation into Daniel's attempted abduction?" she asked.

"We have still not been able to identify the male who we believe drugged Daniel. He was careful to avoid any CCTV, and as you know left the scene as soon as the Police arrived. We believe that he was attempting to deliver Daniel to someone in Heels Bar that night. We have managed to secure a list of everyone who signed in from opening time until just after Daniel was arrested. Rangers are working their way through that now."

"Forward the list to me please. The sooner that we identify the attempted abductor, the sooner we will know what they wanted with Daniel."

"Do you have any theories? Do you think that someone is after one of the specimens?" asked Aidan.

"No, not the specimens. I hope I'm wrong, but I suspect that someone has learned of the existence of the book," replied Esther in a resigned tone.

Esther left the conference room and headed to the first-floor restaurant area; she wanted a quiet coffee before her meeting with Daniel. She never ceased to be impressed with the IES building. It was an amazing juxtaposition of glass and chrome design with beautiful well-maintained botanical areas. The entire building was powered by renewable energy with deep thermal shafts providing heating during winter and cool air in the hotter months. The laboratories on the third and fourth floors all had state of the art equipment relating to their field of study. Esther always found it amusing to watch the faces of newly recruited scientists when they first walked into the laboratory. Like kids in a sweetshop she thought to herself. Ranger control located on the fifth floor monitored everything that happened within the building. They also had remote access to any corresponding system in any country. They were the sentinels of the projects. The sixth floor housed Eden control and maintained contact with all the Edens around the globe. Access was restricted to very few and was heavily guarded by the Rangers. Locations of the Edens were top secret, known only to staff with the highest security clearance. Esther made her way to the seventh floor where Daniel's office was situated. Daniel was standing at the window looking out across the city as Esther entered.

"How did the meeting go?" Daniel asked without turning around.

"Everything is in hand and we are ahead of schedule. The Americans are thinking of pulling out, they are worried since the accident in October. Sonia and the American field crew are happy with our setup so maybe a word of re-assurance from you would sway them. In addition, the Chinese and South Americans insist on accompanying their specimens throughout, Aidan is fine with that," she replied.

"I realise that the maids are extremely dangerous and difficult to control, I also understand the Americans' concern, but Sonia must be given access. I will discuss it with them. Has Aidan provided an update?" asked Daniel, turning to face Esther.

"Aidan has obtained a list of everyone at the club that night and his team are working through it. I have asked that he send me a copy. You still can't remember anything about him?"

57

"I was just drinking a coffee across the road in Jenna's Restaurant, I vaguely remember speaking to a Ranger, and then being with these two men who I did not know trying to get me into the club."

Esther continued, "Unfortunately, the restaurant had no CCTV and you were not captured leaving on any other local security systems, but staff in the restaurant did say that they thought you left with a man in uniform. Aidan has checked and no Rangers spoke to you in the restaurant. The club state their CCTV was not working that night and the doorman no longer works for them. I think the whole thing is very odd. I suspect that someone has knowledge of the book. Sonia has asked whether it will be at the Exhibition Centre, I told her that I am against it. Have you decided yet?"

"I agree with you Esther, information has been leaked, and you must locate the source of that leak. Rule number one. Existence of the Edens must never be disclosed to the general population. You understand the consequences if this were to happen. Tell them that the book will be present but for one day only."

"But surely for that very reason the book should not be allowed to leave here. I strongly urge you to reconsider." she said, clearly agitated.

"The Rangers have failed to make any progress in their investigation, days have now passed. We need something to draw whoever is responsible out into the open," replied Daniel in an assertive voice.

"What about the four from Limehouse?" asked Daniel.

"We are continuing to monitor them and so far, they have said nothing. If that changes, I will let you know immediately," she replied.

"I will speak with the Americans but tell Sonia not to worry it will be here."

***

One evening some months later Daniel received a phone call.

"Good evening Daniel this is Ranger control. We have some news for you about Carla Brown."

Chapter 9

Months after the encounter with Daniel and subsequently to the meeting with Esther, the memories of that night began to fade. The officers were all just relieved that nothing came of the threats and they were all quite happy not to discuss what had happened. Besides, who would believe them, people would think they were mad. Carla was fitting in well at the station and had taken up DI Burns' offer of working in the VSO. DS Carter was her line manager and she appreciated his laid-back approach to life, as he combined it very well with a mix of experience, knowledge and a quirky sense of humour. Simon was a dream to work for, he was always immaculately dressed and smelt of expensive after shave. It transpired that DI Burns and DS Carter had read her initial application to join the Police and had seen her reasons, hence wanting to give her the opportunity to work with them. She really enjoyed being part of the team and kept in touch with Melanie although as they worked on different shifts and different days it was not that often. It had been a particularly cold winter and both Betty and Carla had on occasions suffered from nasty colds but by February the weather had changed for the better. It began to get warmer and they had both shaken off their illnesses. Carla had been invited to an evening drink to celebrate Melanie's birthday. It was on a Thursday night in The Star and she had been looking forward to it for weeks. Before leaving for work that day Carla told Betty that she may be a little late because of the party. She took a change of clothes with her so that she did not have to go home and could go straight to the drink. As she left the office Carla rang Betty just to check that Irene was with her. Irene Porter was their neighbour, she sadly lost her husband early in the previous January, following a long illness. Betty had been there for her and was helping her get through her bereavement. Irene became a regular visitor and they were good company for one another in the evenings when Carla was working. Reassured that Betty was okay, and that Irene was there she made her way to The Star. Carla had a great time at the party. She spent the evening chatting and laughing with colleagues until at around 12:30 am she decided that it was time to go home. After wishing Melanie a final happy birthday she picked up her coat and set off on the journey home. As she waited for the number 15 bus outside the graveyard, her mind briefly returned to the events of 'that' night. After a few moments the bus arrived and Carla boarded, she immediately forgot all about the incident. She considered calling Betty to let her know that she was on her way home but then decided not to bother as she knew that she would be asleep and did not want to wake her. At Watney Street Market she got off the bus and set off walking towards the flat, checking her phone for messages and Facebook. To her surprise she saw lots of missed calls from Irene. Carla had turned her phone to silent when Melanie's speeches started, and she had forgotten to turn the volume back on. She was immediately filled with alarm and began to run home as she called Irene.

"Hello Irene it's me Carla. What's wrong!" she asked breathlessly.

"Oh, Carla I've been trying to call you all night. It's Betty, she's been taken ill. I'm at The East London with her now. Please hurry." replied Irene tearfully.

"What's happened? What's wrong with her?" asked Carla, her voice shaking in fear.

"I think she has had a stroke, but they won't tell me anything as I am not her next of kin. She looks very poorly. Please just hurry. Where are you now?"

"I'm almost home I will get a cab straight away."

"Mrs Reynolds and her husband from the next landing up are waiting for you at the flat in case you came home. They will drive you here. Just hurry please Carla," said Irene desperately.

"I'm on my way."

Carla put her phone back in her pocket and ran towards the flat where she saw Mrs Reynolds waiting in the street. She jumped into the car and they drove to the hospital, a five-minute journey.

Recognising the symptoms of a stroke, Irene had called the ambulance as soon as she saw Betty's condition. She reassured her and kept her awake until the ambulance arrived, then accompanied her to the hospital. On arrival, Betty was rushed into the emergency treatment room whilst Irene was led to the waiting area. Irene had been waiting for what seemed like an eternity when the nurse came through and told her that she could go and sit with Betty by her bed. Betty was asleep with a tube in her arm and a dozen wires attached to a heart monitor by her bedside. Irene held her hand and prayed that Carla would get there soon. She had been sitting with Betty for about an hour when a young man accompanied by a tall slender lady came to the bedside. He was in his mid-twenties with dark hair and she was aged about the same, she was noticeably tall and thin with long blonde hair.

"How is she doing?" he asked.

"I don't know, the doctors won't tell me anything. I'm sorry I don't think I know you." replied Irene.

"My name is Daniel, and this is my wife. I'm Betty's nephew, we came as soon as we heard."

62

"I'm Irene, Betty's neighbour. Betty has never mentioned you. I am sorry. I have been trying to get hold of Carla but she's not answering her phone," said Irene sounding exasperated.

"Me too, but with no luck. Do you mind if we have a moment alone with her?"

"No. No, not at all. I will go get us some coffee and try Carla again," replied Irene, grateful for a reason to stretch her legs.

Irene got up from her chair and walked away from the bed leaving the couple with Betty. She took out her phone and called Carla again. As she waited for Carla to answer she glanced back, looking in the direction of Betty's bed, where Daniel and his wife were standing. Irene saw his wife take a small box from her pocket and open it. The box appeared to change colour slightly, from brown to green, as she dipped her fingers into the contents and then rubbed Betty's forehead. Carla was still not answering her phone, so Irene left another message and made her way to get the coffees. Whilst she was standing at the coffee machine Carla finally answered. Irene gave her the details of the ward and explained where she was. Relieved that Carla was finally on her way she returned to Betty, Daniel and his wife. She handed them a coffee each and sat down.

"I finally got through to Carla, she should be here soon, our neighbour is driving her," announced Irene with a visible expression of relief on her face.

"Thank goodness for that," said Daniel.

"I couldn't help notice, but what did you rub on Betty's forehead?" asked Irene. "I hope you don't mind me asking?"

"Oh that. It is Betty's favourite balm. We thought the smell might comfort her," replied Daniel.

Irene thought it odd that Daniel's wife never spoke a word or even looked in her direction. She just stood there holding Betty's hand.

"Well I will go down and meet Carla if you don't mind waiting here. I will bring her straight up to Betty," said Irene.

"Yes, please do, we will wait with her," replied Daniel.

Irene went outside and waited. It wasn't long before Mr Reynolds pulled up, Carla jumped out of the car and ran towards Irene.

"Where is she? Is she ok?" Carla asked frantically.

"She is upstairs in a bed recovering. The doctors won't tell me anything I'm sorry. Come with me I'll take you. Her nephew and his wife are with her," said Irene as they headed inside.

"Nephew? What nephew? She doesn't have a nephew." Carla replied in surprise.

"He said his name was Daniel. He is with his wife."

Daniel. It can't be. What is he doing here? Carla thought to herself as she hurriedly made her way to the ward.

When they reached Betty's bed there was no trace of Daniel or his wife, the two coffee cups remained on the bedside table. Carla gently took hold of Betty's hand and kissed it. An overwhelming feeling of guilt engulfed her for leaving Betty. Irene explained that they were watching television when Betty complained of feeling unwell. She noticed that her speech was slurred, and one side of her face was dropping. She recognised the symptoms immediately as her late husband also suffered from a stroke. Carla hugged Irene in gratitude, realising that her actions had probably saved Betty's life. As Carla wondered about what the future held the doctor entered the room and walked over to Betty's bed.

"My name is Carla, I'm Betty's granddaughter. Can you tell me how she is?" asked Carla.

"Hello Carla, my name is Doctor Millbank. Your grandma has suffered a major stroke. The good news is that due to Irene's quick response we have been able to prevent any further serious damage. The bad news is that the stroke was significant and will have life changing effects, it is unlikely that she will be able to use her left arm fully, if at all and her speech will be laboured. We will know more in the morning."

"May I stay with her tonight doctor?" asked Carla.

"If you wish of course you can. I will have someone bring you a blanket and pillow for the chair," he replied.

"Doctor one more thing. My friend said that a man and a woman claiming to be his wife came. He said that he was Betty's nephew. Betty doesn't have a nephew. Do you know who they were?" although Carla asked the question, she suspected that she already knew who he was.

"I'm sorry it's so busy here, most people just come in and go straight to the ward. I can assure you that we have not informed anyone that Betty was here," he replied as he turned to leave.

"I'm sorry Carla, I had no idea he wasn't Betty's nephew, otherwise I would have said something," said Irene, looking concerned.

"Don't worry Irene it's not your fault. I just thank God you were there when it happened, I dread to imagine it if she were alone. Thank you so much for taking care of her."

Irene continued. "There was one thing. When I left them to go and get the coffee, I tried to call you again. Whilst I was on the phone, I noticed that the woman rubbed cream onto Betty's forehead. Daniel said it was her favourite balm."

Carla looked at Betty's forehead, she couldn't see a trace of anything. Favourite balm, gran doesn't have a favourite balm Carla thought to herself.

"Irene, what did they look like?" asked Carla.

"Well Daniel had black wavy hair about 5' 11". Oh, and he had a scar on the top of his forehead. She was very tall, over 6' I'd say wearing a long white dress and long green coat. She had long blonde hair almost down to her waist and she was very thin. You know she was almost, well, almost Angelic."

Carla thanked Irene again and although she offered to stay Carla reassured her that everything would be fine and that she should go home and get some rest. Carla promised to call Irene if anything changed. Irene gave Carla a hug and promised to come back tomorrow with some clean clothing and toiletries for Betty. As she sat by Betty's bedside Carla wondered why Daniel had been to the hospital and who the woman was. How did he know that Betty was there before she did? She decided that she would call Matt tomorrow and let him know because the only thing that she could think of was that they were under some form of surveillance.

Carla hardly slept a wink that night, the chair was not particularly comfortable and there always seemed to be an alarm sounding somewhere. The following morning, she was coming back from the bathroom when she noticed a doctor at Betty's bedside. He was chatting with Betty who was now awake and sitting up. Carla walked over and gave Betty a hug, she was surprised at how well she looked.

"Oh, Gran I've been so worried. How are you feeling?" said Carla as tears began to fill her eyes.

"I feel fine sweetheart I don't know what all the fuss is about," replied Betty, noticing that Carla was becoming visibly upset.

"I thought I'd lost you," said Carla, no longer able to hold back her tears.

"Come here sweetheart. I'm not going anywhere yet." Betty replied as she held Carla in her arms.

"Doctor Patel how is she?" asked Carla, having discreetly read the name badge on his coat.

"I need to do some more tests, but Betty has made a good recovery," he replied. "In fact, I have never seen anything like it. It is almost as if she had never suffered a stroke at all. Betty I will be back in about an hour but for now just rest and get something to eat."

Carla telephoned Simon to explain the situation and let him know that she would not be able to work today. As she predicted to herself, he told her to take as much time as she needed and deal with the paperwork on her return to work. She then telephoned DI Burns and told him what had happened at the hospital. He reassured her and told her that he, Simon and Melanie would come to the hospital later that day to see her.

Irene arrived at about 9:30 am with some clean clothing and toiletries for Betty. The two of them sat at her bedside. As they were chatting Doctor Patel came over.

"Good morning Betty. How are you feeling?"

"I feel absolutely fine doctor, in fact I feel very good. When can I go home?"

"Well our tests show that you have made a complete recovery. I must say I cannot explain it, but you can go home whenever you are ready. For the next twenty four hours I want someone to be with you at home at all times, and if you feel at all unwell you must call 999 immediately."

"I will be at home with her, and Irene will be helping me. I've taken some compassionate leave from work." explained Carla.

Following Doctor Patel's visit Betty got herself dressed and Carla called for a taxi. Once they got home Carla again called DI Burns to explain they were back at the flat but as she had not slept well, she wanted to get some rest and that she would see them later that evening. DI Burns told her how glad he was that Betty was home but expressed his surprise at how quickly she had recovered. Immediately following her call with DI Burns her mobile rang again. This time it was DS Carter. "Hello Carla, Simon here."

"Hello Sarge"

"Hope you and your gran are okay. I am just ringing to say that if there is anything that you need whilst you are off please just call me. You have my number. Lifts to hospitals, anything like that, you know where I am. Please do not be embarrassed, just ring me. Look after yourselves."

"Thanks so much for your offer, I appreciate it."

Carla left Betty and Irene in the living room and went off to bed. As she drifted off to sleep, she could not help but wonder what Daniel had done for Betty as she was sure he was responsible for her unexplained recovery.

Chapter 10

Later that afternoon Carla suddenly woke with a start. She had not set her alarm clock and was surprised to see that it was five o'clock. The night spent in the hospital had worn her out as she had so little sleep. As she jumped out of bed her immediate thoughts were with Betty and how she was feeling. To her surprise Betty and Irene were in the kitchen busily preparing dinner. It was incredible how well she looked considering what had happened to her. Carla promised her that she would not be late back and would be home in time for stew. Irene reassured Carla that she was going to stay with Betty until she got back so Carla called DS Carter and arranged a time to meet him and the DI. Rather than meet at the station they arranged to meet at La Serra, an Italian restaurant tucked away in Limehouse, DI Burns, DS Carter and Melanie were already sitting at a table when she arrived. Carla explained what had happened to Betty yesterday and how not only was she sure Daniel had something to do with it but was convinced that all four of their movements were being tracked. Carla's suspicions were proved correct when Daniel walked into the restaurant with another man dressed in a black uniform with green piping. Daniel walked over to their table whilst the other man waited by the door.

"Good evening," said Daniel as he surveyed the quartet.

The four of them just looked at him not sure what to say. Carla eventually broke the silence.

"Good evening. Daniel isn't it?"

"Yes, I am Daniel. I know that you probably have a lot of questions, and I appreciate that you haven't said anything to anyone."

"We didn't really have much choice did we as Esther made perfectly clear," replied DI Burns, clearly slightly annoyed.

"I'm sorry about that but don't be too hard on Esther, she had good reason."

"So, you have been watching us." said Carla.

Daniel did not reply but took four passes on lanyards from his pocket. They were identification passes for IES Exhibition Centre and contained their names and photographs.

"Come along next week, the date and location are on the pass, and I will try and explain everything. Don't worry about work that day, you will find you have already been assigned a training day." With that he turned and made his way towards the restaurant exit.

"Thank you for what you did for Betty." Carla called out.

Daniel turned and smiled as both men left the restaurant.

They each examined their pass which gave them access to the International Environmental Services Exhibition Centre in Greenwich it also included access to restricted seminars and secure areas.

"Environmental seminars? Well that clears everything up," said Melanie sarcastically.

"I think it might be interesting actually. I was a bit of a botanical boffin at University," said DI Burns. He had the intonation in his voice which was clearly intended to surprise.

"I had no idea you were into plants boss." said Melanie smiling at him. None of them had any idea that DI Burns' real passion was botany. At the stage in his life that he needed a career the Police were fast tracking graduate entrants, and the salary was substantially higher than that for budding botanists.

"It's weird isn't it. I mean he looks so normal. I mean compared to what you imagine a botany student to look like," said Carla. "I always imagined scruffy beards, long hair, dirty fingernails, ill-fitting home knitted jumpers ..."

"Yes, he does but he is also cute. Not at all geeky. Don't you think," replied Melanie.

"I guess he is." quipped Carla.

"Excuse me, I am sitting here, let's see what happens when we get there next week," said DI Burns as he blushed and placed his pass in his pocket.

"No offence boss but looking at a load of plants is not my idea of a good time," replied Melanie, also placing her pass in her pocket.

"Somehow I think there's going to be more to it than that," said Simon who had been quietly taking in what had been happening. "If they have gone to the extent of keeping four of us under surveillance, when we don't actually know anything anyway, there must be something important behind it all. I think it will be more than just a convention of Percy Thrower look-alikes."

The restaurant was a large ground floor establishment with a curved bar running half of the length of the room at which several customers were sitting on stools chatting. The tables were intimate and laid out to cater for parties of two, four or six. Ambient lighting added to a relaxing environment. As you entered on the right there was a small stage and a black grand piano. A man in his forties was playing a selection of swing numbers, accompanied by a singer wearing a dinner jacket and bow tie.

As Daniel left, Jaz, the restauranteur came over to their table. Jaz was a smartly dressed dark skinned Mediterranean looking man in his fifties. He had long hair for his age, with a kind

71

but knowledgeable look in his eyes "Has anybody served you yet my friends?" as he surveyed the empty table in front of them.

Before any of them could reply, "Oi, service," he shouted in the direction of one of the waiters.

The unfortunate waiter was Enrique, a balding middle-aged man rather overweight and a bit scruffy looking. His Italian good looks had abandoned him long ago.

"Look. Two beautiful ladies, two handsome men. They need drinks and menus?"

"What is the matter?" Enrique asked quizzically in his Italian accent, tilting his head to one side.

"No! No! You stupid donkey. They have no drinks and no menus," shouted Jaz.

"I was busy."

"Busy? Busy? Give them some menus, take their order and fetch them some drinks!"

Enrique hurried towards the kitchen and shortly later arrived back at the table with four menus. "Please may I take your drinks orders?" he said as he took out his note pad. "Gin and tonic please," replied Carla. "Same for me," replied Melanie." "Orange juice for me," said Simon. "Driving duties again." "Same here," replied DI Burns. "On call later."

"Enrique make sure that you bring these lovely ladies some flowers." said Jaz as he left their table.

"He's a bit mean to his staff," said Carla.

"It's all play acting Carla. It's like being part of the cabaret getting served in here. It's like this all the time. You do realise that we are going to have to have a go at the karaoke later?" said Melanie looking at the DI as if to say "How about you?"

"I would love to, but I have to get home at a reasonable time as I am on call. Simon is my driver again tonight, so he is also out of the running. I'm sure you two will have a great time."

As he finished speaking the drinks arrived. Enrique also placed a plate of pizza slices on the table. "Pizza on the house," he said as he put the plate down.

The four of them drank their drinks and ate their snack as they discussed the type of song that each could sing.

"Okay we need to be on our way really. Give my best to Betty please," said DI Burns as they got up to leave.

"I will. Goodnight."

"So, you up for a song later Carla?"

"Why not? I will just call Betty to make sure she's okay." Carla replied. She called home and spoke to Betty who told her that she was fine and that she should have fun but not to forget that she had stew waiting in the oven.

Enrique then returned to the table and gave the girls a rose each. "Jaz wants to know, would you like a cocktail on the house?" he said, notebook in hand. "That would be lovely," said Melanie. "Two champagne cocktails please."

A few minutes later Jaz arrived at the table with three cocktails. He sat down in DI Burns' seat as he handed them their drinks. "Cheers," he said enthusiastically as he raised his glass.

The three laughed and chatted a while, Jaz flirted relentlessly, but in a very charming way before he stood up. "Nice to meet you ladies. Have a lovely evening," he said as he walked across the restaurant to berate another waiter at another table.

At just before nine o'clock the singer announced that his spot was complete but that the karaoke would be starting shortly hosted by Dommy Natricks. "An unusual name," commented Melanie. A few moments later the karaoke started. The girls both looked the host up and down, then looked at one another and giggled. It was clearly a drag queen. "You can tell by the hands and the Adam's apple," said Carla knowledgably. He was wearing a long blue sequined dress with a split up the side and a blonde wig. Between singers he told inappropriate jokes and was generally very amusing.

The two of them sang a few numbers before both agreeing not to give up their day jobs. They went over and sat at the bar whilst finishing their final drink, waiting to settle the bill before setting off home. As they waited a man who had been standing with three others walked over to Carla. He was obviously drunk.

"You're a good singer," he said to Carla.

"I don't think it was me you were listening to," replied Carla modestly.

"No, you are really. Can I buy you a drink?" he said, as he briefly turned his head and smiled in the direction of his friends.

"No thanks. We are just going," said Carla.

"Oh, go on, just one," he slurred.

"The lady said no thanks, so please go back to your friends." Melanie interrupted.

"Oh, I see. This your girlfriend. Come back with me, I will change your mind," he man said as he gently patted Carla's bottom.

Melanie moved so fast that he didn't see what was coming. Discreetly she took his right hand and positioned it in a grip that her father had taught her, and she squeezed his knuckles together. The man shouted in pain as he fell to his knees.

"Apologise to the lady," said Melanie as she squeezed his hand tighter. The man shouted out in pain. "I'm sorry! I'm sorry!"

"Now you are going to get up, and you and your friends are going to leave." ordered Melanie releasing his hand.

He rubbed his hand and walked back over to where his friends were standing.

"Come on guys, let's get out of this dyke bar," he said as they left. It was loud and clearly intended for the girls to hear.

"Impressive move Mel. You know I could have just nicked him myself?"

"Yes, but do you really want to spend the next three hours in the custody suite?"

"I guess not," she replied.

"Right, Enrique has offered a shot of Sambuca on the house, one more shot and then home. Okay?" asked Melanie.

"Okay."

They drank their shots and as they were getting off their stools to leave Jaz walked over. He had noticed what happened from the other end of the restaurant. The men had left before he reached Carla and Melanie.

"You want a job here?" Jaz said to Melanie with a broad grin.

They both laughed, finished dismounting their stools and left the restaurant.

Chapter 11

Esther was sitting in her office reading through the final reports from the various IES directorates. The exhibition was due to start the following day, and everything was running on schedule. She had personally supervised the connection of the American pod to the Exhibition Centre, and the exhibit was now safely stored in its temporary habitat. All of the other exhibits had arrived and had been placed in their respective cabinets. Oliver Chambers, Sonia Fielding and Kevin Hart were still present at the Centre going through last minute checks ensuring that everything was ready. Esther had other things on her mind. Aidan had sent her the list of names from Heels Bar and she had gone through them all. She didn't recognise any of them although she realised that some of them may be fake. She was hoping that she would recognise one from her time in MI5 and MI6. She had requested a report into the accident in America the previous October involving the maid, it had arrived that morning and she had just opened it on her laptop when Daniel walked into her office.

"Good morning Esther."

"Good morning Daniel."

"How is everything Esther? Are we ready?"

"Everything is ready," she replied. "I still don't agree with you inviting those four or the book being present. Oh, and by the way, I heard about your little hospital visit. Both of you going with no Ranger protection? Are you insane? After all that's happened."

"It was an unplanned last-minute visit. There was no time. Besides the way we travelled nobody saw us," he replied.

"Please don't do anything like that again Daniel. At least not until I find out who's behind what's going on," she said sternly.

"Any luck with that?" he asked.

"Nothing on the list. I have just received the report from the States about the accident. I was just about to read it."

"Terrible thing that. I must say I was surprised it happened," said Daniel.

"Me too. They have the pictures of the poor Rangers here," as she showed Daniel the screen.

"That's him! That's the guy who drugged me! I remember his face now," said Daniel as he studied the photograph.

Chapter 12

Don Magarde joined the United States Army when he was nineteen years old. After serving several tours in Afghanistan he quickly rose through the ranks to Corporal and had spent his last three years working in electronic and cyber warfare. He married when he was twenty-three years old, and a year later his wife had a beautiful daughter. He was happy with his life, he had a lovely wife, a job that he loved, a beautiful little girl and another baby on the way. All that changed one summer afternoon when his wife was involved in a car crash and was tragically killed along with their unborn child. The only thing that kept him going was his daughter Corin who, because of his job, now lived with his parents. Then as if he were suddenly being denied any happiness by some unseen force, tragedy struck again. Corin developed an extremely rare lung disease for which there was no known cure. Don decided to leave the army at the age of twenty-seven so that he could spend more time taking care of her. An ex-army friend had offered him a job in his IT company. The pay was good and covered Corin's medical expenses. Don had been in his new job for about a month when he was contacted by Tom Walker, another former army colleague who wanted to meet and catch up. The two of them met in a bar not too far from Don's home. It was good to talk about old times, however the conversation then moved on to something that was to change his entire career path. Out of the blue Tom said. "Don, I am aware of a job vacancy that would suit you perfectly. It is within the security sector. Recruitment is carried out by personal recommendation. The job title is Ranger. What do you think?"

After receiving a very vague rundown on the role from Tom, Don agreed to attend a meeting at the IES Research Centre in Half Moon Bay, California to discuss the offer. If what Tom had said was correct, this would be perfect for him. It offered full relocation to California, all expenses paid, an excellent salary and most important of all first-class medical treatment would be available for Corin. It became very apparent to Don that IES had been watching him for some time as they knew everything about him. It dawned on him that Tom Walker had not contacted him randomly, but that he had been the subject of a targeted recruitment process. At the meeting they told him that if he agreed to work for them the training would be tough but more importantly, it would become his life. The ideals that they endeavoured to achieve had more significance than he could guess, it would be the most important job of his life. He would be working with a group of committed people on a joint mission. A mission so important that if they failed, the future of the human race was at risk.

Don decided to accept the job offer. The training was extremely intense covering all the usual security areas including combat, psychological warfare and firearms training. The recruits were given general overviews of some of the areas in which the scientists worked. Don found these fascinating. It became clear that the work involved improving the environment and he was impressed by the levels of commitment demonstrated by the scientists, who seemed to work as if they had a deadline to meet. The Rangers role was to protect the personnel of IES especially the scientists, in addition to all IES buildings. Training made it clear that they were so important that if necessary, Rangers should protect them with their lives. Although during the initial training phases, information about IES and its purpose was mostly withheld, this changed as over time he began to get invitations to a selection of update meetings. It became apparent that the main area of research for the staff here was plastic reduction in water. Don completed his training and was enjoying his time with IES, he had always made friends easily, and he fitted in well. He formed a particularly close friendship with a field crew research scientist named Ellie Hammond. Most of her work was based in Half Moon Bay and over time they had become close. Don had taken Ellie to meet his parents, and even to visit Corin. Don knew that there were many other areas of activity at IES, some areas that he did not have access to, and some areas that he had not known existed. He was also aware that due to her particular skill set and experience, Ellie had access to all areas. Although he was curious, he knew the IES position on information sharing, and did not discuss any aspect of her work with her. One of the clear rules was that you did not share information about your work with anyone, not even family.

All that changed one Monday morning when Don was called into the senior Ranger's office. He was informed that had impressed them, he had passed all the training requirements and that later he would be fully appraised of the work and given full access to all areas. This included the area behind the large steel doors on minus one level which he had wondered about for so long. The senior Ranger explained that he would be taken to the lower levels and shown around after which he would attend a seminar on the top floor which would fully explain the purpose of IES. After collecting their firearms, both made their way to the lower level. Outside the large doors below the CCTV cameras stood two armed Rangers. The door was opened by fingerprint recognition. As the senior Ranger placed his finger on the reader alarms sounded and red lights flashed as the doors slowly opened. They entered a long corridor with white walls, grey floor and low lighting. The aroma of the sea filled the air. At the end of the corridor were two smaller swing doors, on the other side was a large semi-circular observation deck which protruded from the cliff face. It contained computers and large video screens; the walls were entirely glass. At either side of the room was a lift which ran down to a wall-enclosed area by the shore. From the observation area Don could see that beyond the walled area there was a vast area of sea which had a large fence circling it. This was obviously designed to contain something big and strong.

One of the screens clearly displayed a map of the shoreline, the outline of the wall, and the outline of the pen in the sea beyond. It showed objects moving around as if they were being tracked, there were about thirty green dots on the screen. Whilst Don stood taking in all that he was looking at, the senior Ranger had been speaking to one of the scientists when he turned and called for Don to join him. All three entered the lift to the right of the room, once again alarms sounded as the lift door opened. The lift descended and the three exited. The scientist walked towards the wall where there was a control panel and a metal shutter above it. He placed his finger on the reader and the control panel activated. He pressed a further button and the shutter slowly began to rise. As it got higher Don saw that behind it was a glass panel with a view of the shoreline. He then saw something large and grey rise slightly from the ocean then disappear below the water line. The scientist pressed some buttons on the control panel which influenced whatever was in the water because it began to move towards the shore. Don stared in disbelief as he saw what emerged from the water and began crawling onto the beach. The creature had a large head about two feet wide, two black eyes and a mouth almost the same width as the head which was full of pointed teeth. The nose comprised two small holes and it appeared to have a black mane of hair running from its head down its back which extended to a long tail, like an eel. It pulled itself out of the water with its two muscular arms which had webbed hands and large claws. Its skin was grey apart from its back which was a light pink, almost the same colour as human skin. The creature emerged completely from ocean onto the beach, moving around like a snake. It raised its head as if sniffing the air. The scientist explained that he had produced the sound of an injured animal which attracted it out of the ocean. The maids, as he called them, prefer to eat warm bloodied mammals. He described how they have a most interesting way of attracting their prey. The maids have gills on their head but also along the body. This allows the top half of the body to remain out of the water. When hungry they raise the top half above the water line and pull in their arms and head exposing just the pink skin and black hair. They then whimper like an injured animal or a lost young one. This attracts would-be predators. Their excellent sense of smell alerts them once the prey is near, they then turn and bite into the prey before dragging it under the water. He went on to say that it is believed that these creatures were the origins of myths such as sirens or mermaids. Don was fascinated but also terrified at the thought. This maid was at least fifteen feet long and he had never seen anything so frightening in his life. The creature eventually slid back into the sea and was gone. The scientist closed the metal screen and they all returned to the observation area. Don was amazed at what he had just seen and was eager to get to the seminar room where he was told all of his questions would be answered.

Don had always been under the impression that IES had been conceived as an international government initiative to combat global issues. In reality, that was what the scientists were all working to achieve. He had no concept of the importance of success or what force had motivated governments to work so closely together to achieve this goal.

As Don entered the seminar room, he saw that there were two other men already seated, he later established that they were newly recruited scientists engaged in the field of plastic pollution. The senior Ranger and a middle-aged female were sitting at the front of the room. One by one she looked intently at the three of them.

Chapter 13

The female approached the lectern and surveyed the assembled audience. "Ladies and gentlemen. My name is Alison Baker, I am head of human resources. I am going to tell you an amazing story which will explain why IES exists around the world and how important its work is for the future of the human race." She explained that on the morning of the 23rd June 1908 a top Russian scientist was visited by a young man with a simple message. 'Man is poisoning this planet and it will not be tolerated. Change your behaviour or face the consequences. A warning will be sent on the 30th June at a place you call Tunguska.' The scientist passed the message to the Russian government, but they did not take it seriously. The 30th of June arrived and as promised, something inexplicable happened. With no further warning or explanation, two thousand square kilometres of forest was wiped out in an instant with the force of two thousand Hiroshima bombs. A few days later the young man visited the scientist again with a further message. 'We will not interfere with your destiny as long as you begin to repair the damage you have done to the planet. We will be watching you.' Over the following years many countries set up their own research departments to combat the pollutants that were causing the damage. As the years passed the countries involved in the work communicated less frequently and some even gave up on the research. Tunguska became a distant memory. As technology advanced countries became more self-isolating and wars broke out. The message from the young man had been long forgotten, however some countries persisted in their work. Only because of this, the world was given a second chance but this time it was under the supervision of a group of Ambassadors. Their role was to hold a world overview and guide people in the right direction if necessary.

On the morning of the 15th March 1990 a young man walked into the Ministry of Defence building in London. He said to the receptionist. "Good morning, my name is Ezra. Could you please ask whoever is in charge here if they have noticed the asteroid yet? I will sit down and wait for a reply." The receptionist thought that this was rather odd and called security who initially thought him another eccentric. Just as they took hold of him to escort him from the building, he said "If you care about all the people you love you will deliver my message." The security guard that had hold of him at the time took this as a threat and Ezra was detained however his message was reported. Within minutes of hearing this, a senior member of the military came down to see him. What nobody except a few people around the world knew, was that an asteroid the size of Mount Everest had inexplicably changed trajectory and was on a collision course with Earth. It was destined to collide in seven days. Ministry of Defence officials initially assumed that he must be an amateur astronomer and that he had somehow spotted the asteroid. Their opinions changed when he told them that the Tunguska warning had gone unheeded, and this was their last chance to remedy matters. They had to come up with a credible plan to stop devastating the world's environment. He told them that pre identified species on earth would be protected but that humans would be removed. He gave them two days to bring the world leaders to a meeting point where rules needed to be laid down. Failure to do so would lead to the elimination of humans. He informed them that he would return immediately before the collision was due to happen, by that time they needed to have a workable plan. They would be informed of the location closer to the time. Ezra was then locked in a secure room whilst officials considered the best way to deal with this. When they returned to the room he had inexplicably vanished. There was no damage to the room, and there was no possible escape route. Scientists had no explanation for the asteroid course change and there was nothing that they could do to alter the course or stop it. It was agreed that the public would not be notified of the impending collision due to the panic and chaos that would follow. After initial resistance from world leaders and politicians, most of whom considered themselves too important to be told what to do, they decided that they had no choice but to formulate a way forward and meet him again.

The location for the meeting was circulated, it was to be held in London's Albert Hall. Amidst high security the group gathered, their personal grievances with each other temporarily forgotten. They had only one mission, it was vital that they prevented the destruction of mankind by a force that they previously had no idea even existed. The delegates took their allocated seats and waited with their entourages, wondering where this mysterious man was. Suddenly a small circular bright white light appeared a few feet off the floor in the centre of the stage. The circle grew until it was at least twelve feet in diameter. Although it shone brightly it did not hurt the eyes to look at. Then out of the light stepped the young man who had visited The Ministry of Defence on the 15th of March. He was just under six feet tall and appeared around twenty years old, he wore a long white robe with a number of gold symbols running down the left sleeve. He had long brown hair, blue eyes and a light brown complexion. "My name is Ezra, and I have been sent to collect you. All those invited to attend please follow me," he said. He walked back into the light and the invited dignitaries followed him. Some of their staff attempted to follow but were prevented from doing so by an invisible force field. The light then suddenly disappeared, leaving the remaining attendees wondering where their colleagues had gone, and whether they would ever return. After about fifteen minutes the light suddenly reappeared, as quickly as it had vanished, and the leaders emerged looking shocked and they told a fantastic story. They described how as they passed through the circle, they emerged into what they described as another realm. They walked into a field of lush green grass with a clearing, in the middle of a great forest. Above them were two suns which emitted a warm glow. Above the suns they saw planets, moons and stars. The clearing in which they were standing extended outwards for miles. Surrounding them were large black rectangular stones protruding from the ground. All bore gold coloured symbols, hundreds per stone and there were thousands of stones. At the edge of the clearing was a forest with trees hundreds of feet high bearing strange fruits. In the distance were mountain ranges with gushing waterfalls cascading down the rockfaces. It was a beautiful place. The delegates learned new skills including using natural ingredients to build homes, clothe and feed themselves. They were shown how to build houses from a brown powder which was made from the ground skin of a spider then added to water and subsequently set in moulds. The same spider's abandoned webs provided a material that could be woven and was as soft as silk and warm as wool. The race that lived on this planet had technology and obtained their power from a mineral which created no waste or toxic by-products. Marie Duvoux, the French representative, explained to them how a group called the Shey Atar could communicate with all living things, not through normal means but by mystically sending and receiving emotions. Fear, joy, despair, they shared them all with life. They saw many Shey Atar appearing through portholes with an array of bizarre looking companions. They would appear and walk among the stones, the Shey Atar would each be carrying a book which they would then open and as they touched a symbol it would appear on the gold leaf pages. The group of leaders had no concept of how long they had been in the mystical land, they believed they had been there for at least a year, and that the Earth had long been destroyed. One day with no warning, Ezra summonsed them all to a meeting. He told them that they were about to return to their own world where they would find that they had only been gone for fifteen minutes. Everyone was given the option to stay if they wished, one Russian delegate selected this offer and stayed behind, as the remainder of the group followed Ezra back through the circle. Immediately prior to leaving, Ezra gave them a message. The message was simple. "You were warned in 1908 but failed to listen. You cannot be trusted to deal with your own mess. You must work together to remedy the damage you have done to earth. We will not clean up your mess for you. Ambassadors will be assigned to guide you and help where possible, but you will have to fix the damage. There will be rules. Rule 1. Our existence will not be disclosed to your people. Rule 2. The consequences of failure will not be disclosed to your people. Rule 3. Under no circumstances will our symbols be used for harm or profiteering. If you fail in any of these rules mankind will be eliminated. The Shey Atar are the handmaidens of nature. They maintain balance and harmony. Their powers are beyond your comprehension. If a species becomes a threat to the existence of all others the Shey Atar will remove it. They have done this before. You have had your final warning. Take what you have learned here away with you. I will contact you shortly with further instructions. We have altered the course of the asteroid; it will no longer collide with Earth."

"As a result of this amazing occurrence IES was formed and operated all over the world by countries co-ordinating with one another, establishing solutions to fix the environmental damage that had been caused. There were one hundred delegates present at the original meeting, however a smaller steering group of fifteen was formed from within. Members of this group were given the locations of three Edens, created by the Shey Atar which they subsequently helped to fortify. Later, IES would build many more. When an endangered species was identified they were removed from their natural environment and placed in an Eden for protection. An example of this was the maid. They were the last surviving colony and were located off Inagua Island, however they are now located in the IES research centre at Half Moon Bay. It was discovered that they have a remarkable ability to remove plastic micro particles from water. This had been studied for some years but still nobody knows how they do it. When dealing with maids utmost care is needed, they are extremely dangerous, they will tear you to pieces and there will be nothing left of you. So, ladies and gentlemen all we need to do is fix the damage, and then change the habits of the entire population of the world without telling them why or what will happen if they don't. Simple? There is a journal that you should read as soon as you can please. The French representative Marie Duvoux kept a record of her time there and was permitted to bring it back. It is online in the IES library folders. The Journal of Marie Duvoux."

The scientists had some technical questions and Don learned from the answers that they had access to exotic creatures and plant life in the Edens, in addition to symbols provided by an Ambassador. When combined with specific symbols from a book, elements and even atomic structures could be changed. One such discovery was a solution that broke down some toxins in the air

89

to produce rainwater. A covert experiment implementing this process was currently being tested worldwide. Don, amazed by what he had heard, wondered whether there was anything within that book that could help Corin.

Chapter 14

D on inconspicuously continued his work at IES and his relationship with Ellie blossomed. The most dangerous role in the entire complex was changing the water filter in the maids' enclosure. The scientists had installed a pump so that they could extract samples of water to analyse, however the filters often became blocked. When this occurred, Rangers were required to change them. The area around the filter had a glazed door that was closed and locked during this process, thus preventing the maids from gaining access. Just being so close to them terrified Don as they gathered around and watched what was happening intently through the toughened glass screens. Now that Don was now fully accredited Ellie could talk to him freely about the different aspects of her work. Her stories were fascinating, she revealed to Don that during an experiment that she had witnessed, pure water in a gold container was turned into oil. The vessel had to be gold as it was inert, and the symbols had no effect on it. Don commented that if it wasn't for the fact that they were actually trying to stop the use of oil, they had just solved the world's energy problems. Jesus turned water to wine, now we turn water to oil. Don asked how the change occurred. Ellie explained the relevance of the symbols, and that they were allocated to the scientists from a book kept in England by Daniel, the IES Ambassador for the United Kingdom. The book contained symbols originating from the Shey Atar, known as the female handmaidens of nature.

Ellie went on to say "The symbols were examined, and we photocopied them, but only the inscribed symbols in the book were activated during experiments. After analysing the symbols and magnifying by one thousand times we observed a complex pattern structure appear."

Ellie took a sheet of paper and pen and drew a diagonal line and a small circle beneath it.

"This is one of the more simplistic symbols, it looks like a line and a circle however when magnified we found a complex pattern structure forming a coded message remarkably like something along the lines of DNA.

Ellie explained that there were teams of scientists across the entire world working on different projects and that the symbols helped them with their work as they could alter the atomic and molecular structure. She said that all IES research centres worked in harmony, utilising a powerful computer. In turn it created the correct sequence of symbols to match the outcome that they were seeking, however occasionally it did not work as planned. The experiment that resulted in obtaining oil from water, was a prime example of a symbol sequence that did not work as they expected. She went on to say that some symbols needed to be inscribed into a stone and that the stone needed to be positioned over a Ley line for it to work. Other symbols were activated by touch or even just thought. Ellie told Don that she was looking forward to her upcoming trip, as she would be able to see some symbol experiments at first hand. She had visited an Eden during her work as a field crew member and was due to travel to England to escort a maid to an IES exhibition. Daniel allocated the symbols from a book which contained hundreds of designs. Each had a unique ability and when combined they could create unbelievable results. She was excited about the visit to England because she had heard that the book was going to be made available to them. They could finally choose symbols that they believed would help identify the ability that the maids possess to neutralise plastic particles. Don questioned why the Shey Atar would allow the book to be seen by mere humans. Ellie explained that it was not the Shey Atar book, but a book written by one of their students during the 1700's. On rare occasions throughout history the Shey Atar selected students, mostly females, to teach them the ways of nature and how to best utilise the power of the symbols and how to appreciate and be at one with all other life around them. In 1991, during construction work in Canary Wharf, East London three skeletons were uncovered. One was that of an adult female, the other two were younger girls. Buried alongside them was a heavy wooden box which contained a book of many symbols, and a stone with some of these symbols carved into it. Work was immediately halted whilst the Coroner and authorities investigated the find and removed the bodies and box. IES, in turn retrieved the box and book from the Coroner and it is now securely stored in the IES building in London. It is a book compiled by a student of the Shey Atar. Once they arrived at The Mortuary the skeletons were examined, and whilst it was not possible to ascertain how the girls died, the woman appeared to have been burned to death. It is thought that she was probably what was known as a Wiccan and there were many until men decided to burn them as witches. What a terrible way to die, and she was probably only trying to help people. "Sometimes I wonder if we deserve to survive at all?" she said.

Corin's condition continued to deteriorate and Don's continued requests to IES to try and help her were refused. Their reasoning being that it was not what they were created for, and although they sympathised with his problem they could not help. Even when he asked for help raising the one million dollars for experimental treatment in Switzerland it was refused as they said it was highly unlikely that it would assist in her recovery.

Don walked into the hospital and made his way along the myriad of corridors to Corin's room. She lay sleeping as he entered, and Don sat on the chair by her bed and held her hand. He hated the sight of the drips and monitors that surrounded her. How can this be right? How is this fair? She is just a child; she has lost her mother is that not pain enough? Don thought to himself hoping some greater power could read his thoughts. As he sat there considering all this Corin awoke and looked at him.

"Hello princess," said Don quietly.

"Hello daddy," she replied softly.

"How are you feeling today?"

"I'm tired. I want to go home. I don't like it here."

"Very soon princess. Very soon. Right now, you need to rest and become strong." He replied, trying with all his strength to contain the emotions that were searing through his body.

"When daddy?"

"Soon Corin, daddy needs to go away for a while to find the medicine you need to make you better again. Corin no matter what anybody tells you, I promise I will come back and take you home. Do you understand?"

"I don't want you to go Daddy." She said with tears in her eyes.

"I know princess. Daddy doesn't want to go either, but I have to get your medicine. Besides grandma and grandpa are going to be with you every day until I come back."

"Please don't leave me daddy. I don't want you to go." Corin replied, now crying.

Don's heart was breaking, he was struggling to hold back the tears, he did not ever want to leave her, but he had to go, it was the only option that was open to him.

"Corin. Corin look at me. Do you remember how we make our promises?" asked Don.

94

Corin looked at him with tears in her eyes and nodded.

Don placed his right hand on his heart and raised his left hand.

"I promise I will come back and take you home and you will be better again."

Corin smiled at him. Don leant over and kissed her on the forehead and told her to get some rest.

Corin gave him a hug, lay back and drifted off to sleep.

Don sat with her until his parents arrived. He gave them a hug, took a long look at Corin sleeping then slipped out.

The treatment was Corin's only chance and Don knew that he had to do something. Many of Don's former army colleagues had moved into close protection work, utilising the skills that they had learnt in the military. They were a sought-after commodity in that sector as they needed little training, and mostly displayed both the disciplined work ethic and camaraderie that the role required. He knew of one that was employed by a Bulgarian businessman who was known only as 'The Bulgarian'. Don recalled that through past conversations that the businessman was involved in trading arms with nations that found it difficult to obtain them using legitimate methods. Whilst he was extremely rich and powerful, if crossed he was also highly dangerous. It occurred to Don that if he could obtain the symbols for the water to oil experiment and sell the formula to The Bulgarian, he may be able to raise sufficient funds for Corin's treatment. He knew that it would be impossible for him to use the formula himself. He possessed neither the equipment to carry out the conversion, nor the contacts to sell it on. He was also aware that his friend's boss had both the finance to purchase the equipment and the contacts that he needed were already in place. He realised that it was a dangerous idea and a betrayal of everything that IES stood for. In contrast, all that mattered to him was obtaining the treatment that Corin needed. It was impossible for him to acquire the symbols as he had no access to the laboratories, but he easily obtained Ellie's computer password. He remembered that she talked about a book in London and how the symbols were allocated to them by Daniel, The Ambassador. Using the stolen password Don logged onto the system, masquerading as Ellie, he then obtained details of the process used and images of the transformation. He copied the data onto a memory stick and logged off the system. After having considered the pros and cons he decided to ask his friend to arrange a meeting in order that he could make the offer to The Bulgarian in exchange for the funds for Corin's treatment. He no longer cared what happened to him, all he cared about was that Corin was given the opportunity to be cured. His friend brokered the meeting, and Don related the fantastic story, showing the images and transcript he had stolen. He thought that they would consider him mad but strangely The Bulgarian believed him. The deal was done but was dependent on Don providing the symbols. The Bulgarian promised to supply all the equipment that was needed but told Don that if he failed to come up with the goods then he and his daughter would both die. Don formulated a plan in his mind, he knew that he had to leave IES and travel to London. Once there, he needed to arrange Daniel's abduction and obtain the symbols or even the book itself. In his mind he started to formulate a plan.

Chapter 15

Don hatched a plan. Using the skills acquired during his military service he assembled an electrical component that would create a power surge, activated by a timer. By placing it in the exact position of the control panel it would look as if the surge had knocked out the door security and CCTV for the maids' compound. He ripped a spare uniform into pieces which he smeared with his own blood, which he had been extracting from himself over a period, using syringes. The timer would give him the opportunity to enter the compound and more crucially be seen on CCTV. He would then need to place his bloodied clothes in the water and escape, as once the surge occurred the maids' door would also become unlocked. He had secreted a motorcycle to affect his escape, it was hidden through a walkway leading to the maids' area, and he planned to disappear that way after retrieving the electrical component. Everyone would think that he was dead and the Rangers would have no need to trace him. Had he simply resigned from IES, the Rangers would track him down and monitor his movements. The morning came when he was going to put his plan into action. Everything was ready, or so he thought. As Don waited to change the filter, Mark Jones, a passing colleague stopped and chatted to him, offering to help him with the operation. Despite Don's best effort to talk him out of it, he had no choice but to allow Mark to assist. Any remonstration would have become suspicious as the task was an onerous one, made so much easier with two people so they both made their way to the maids' enclosure. They entered the enclosure and Mark walked over to the filter control. He looked at Don who was just standing at the door and smiled as he said. "Are you going to help, or are you just going to stand there?" Don looked at him with a blank expression on his face as the lights faded and the door locks clicked open. Mark wondered whether Don was okay, he seemed distant, almost in a trance, he noticed that he was carrying a plastic bag, the contents of which he emptied into the water. Don looked in Mark's direction and said, "I'm so sorry," before running out of the main door and slamming it shut behind him. The maids' compound underwater door slowly dropped open. Mark ran to the door and started banging on it, he was begging Don to open it, but Don held it shut. As he hammered on the door Mark heard the splash of something in the compound water. Don held the door closed, as he listened to Mark's screams then silence apart from the splashing of the maids as they swam around the enclosure.

***

Esther had immediately contacted United States IES and informed them that Daniel had identified Don as one of his kidnappers. The Americans initially thought that Mark and Don's deaths had been a tragic accident caused by a power surge. Consequently, they did not dig too deeply into the cause of the failure. The assumption being that it was obviously a power surge that had knocked out the CCTV and locks, a theory supported by retrieving the burnt-out element. The retrieval of both shredded blood-stained uniforms confirmed that they had both died. On receipt of the update from Esther a forensic investigation was initiated. They discovered the traces of wire and tape fitting that could have held a device in place and from the tape residue they identified Don's DNA. They also found burnt components suggesting something had been attached and caused the surge prior to being removed. This was unquestionably sabotage but by whom? Don was clearly involved but was he working alone, or with an accomplice? Esther ordered that the CCTV images needed to be reviewed using wider parameters than originally thought. If Don were still alive then he would be captured somewhere on the system making good his escape. Sure enough, he was identified leaving through the maids' walkway. A high level covert proactive surveillance operation was authorised. All of Don's known contacts were put under twenty four hour watch, and alerts were placed on all his credit and bank cards, similar tactics were deployed on his mobile phone but there was no trace of him, and no activity on either cards or phone. Esther advised Aidan of what the Americans had discovered, he could not believe that one of their own was responsible. Despite Esther's concerns, Daniel insisted the exhibition went ahead as planned.

Chapter 16

The opening day of the exhibition arrived, and hundreds of people attended, the queue snaked through the barriered entry system. The public area looked amazing with beautiful exhibits, interactive displays and eye-catching demonstrations. IES had opened similar venues all over the world and they were becoming more and more popular. Part of the IES strategy in so doing was to try and change the way in which the world's population viewed saving the environment, and the centres were a huge success in that respect. Their remit covered a wide spectrum of arenas from protecting endangered species to establishing sustainable food sources, tips on improving the environment and even methods of recycling. In the private areas however, scientist and field crews from around the world gathered to learn about the species that were being donated, and how they could help to find the solutions to the problems being researched. Inside the private area Oliver and Sonia took their seats as the first presenter took to the podium. Miss Maria Sanchez was the Professor of Botanical Research at the South American IES Institute. She began by telling them the story of the arrival of the conquistadors in her country. Fuelled by their greed for gold they looted all that they could find. The diseases that they brought with them eventually wiped out an entire race and they never did find the elusive gigantic seam which they believed to be the source of the Incas gold. The Incas took their secret of how they amassed their gold and silver with them to their graves. This was because whilst the raiders were looking to the mountains for the elusive veins of precious metals, the secret lay hidden on the remote banks of the Amazon. Miss Sanchez signalled for her Rangers to remove the curtain from her large display cabinet. Behind it was an artificial fast flowing river with banks on both sides. Kevin and his team had made a good job of making the display appear realistic. Planted on the banks of the river were the exhibits that Maria had brought with her, which would eventually be transferred to the Eden. They were small plants with a single central stalk and smaller stems growing from it, each of which had a single leaf. The most unusual thing about the plant was how it defended itself from the fast-flowing water. There was a mesh of roots in front of the plants, they were coated in a layer of gold. The plant extracted the gold from the flowing water and cemented it in place to create a defence. It had a retractable horizontal tube which when required it would place into the water. This was then filtered, and the plant extracted the nutrients that it needed to survive in addition to the gold that it required for defence. It could also extract silver as it has good healing properties. If the plant became damaged it would extract the silver and secrete it over the wound. When the plant was healed the silver coating would drop off. This was the true source of the Incas gold and silver. What Maria and her team had been trying to do was to create a mutated species of the plant which could extract the heavy and poisonous metals in water. The UK Eden scientists intended to assist with the research. "We call it Planeta Thesaurum Istum, The Treasure Plant and we hope to obtain symbols that can help us with the mutation," she explained.

Maria received a round of applause and as she dismounted the podium the next presenter, the Japanese representative, was introduced.

Akito Nakamura, presenting Japan's extremely rare and deadly exhibit from its Eden approached the podium. Akito told the audience of the exotic plant they discovered many years ago on Mount Fiji. He pointed to the Japanese display cabinet where in the rocky ground was a plant with large flat leaves which were about four feet long. They spread out on the ground from the centre of the plant. In the middle was a brown pod about two feet long. He explained that the plant was currently in its dormant stage. In order to demonstrate its cycle, he had a series of images. The first image was the plant in its current state, as the display progressed the plant evolved. Firstly, the leaves began to rise creating an oval bowl shape. The pod then opened and a single stem full of beautiful fruits rose from within. He explained that the fruits had a strong sweet aroma. Akito then went on to say that the leaves then emitted carbon monoxide gas. The smell of the fruit attracted small mammals, once inside the bowl to feast on the fruits the highly toxic gas killed the animal. The base of the pod then parted, and the dead animal fell inside, the pod closed and absorbed the corpse. It had been established that this particular form of carbon monoxide had a positive effect on surrounding plants. As it was absorbed it caused the surrounding plants to increase in seed production and practically removed all disease. Experiments which involved placing the plant in a field of crops had increased harvest yield by three hundred per cent and almost eradicated disease. This plant meant that there was no longer a need to use any form of pesticide or hormone growth treatment to increase the crop. The only drawback was that the plant very rarely reproduced, only flowering every three to four years, thereby increasing the number of plants required to maintain a constant supply of product. Akito finished by saying that he was offering the exhibit to the UK Eden, in particular to his good friend Oliver who he hoped in turn would find a way to increase its reproductive ability.

The seminars continued apace, introducing a fascinating array of species including the Chinese Tree Spider and the American maid. Scientists and field crews from all over the world discussed theories and the progress that had been achieved with their respective projects. The mood was relaxed, and the organisers were pleased that everything was running smoothly. Esther and Daniel were in the control room when she received a further update from American IES. They advised that they had still found no trace of Don but informed her that he had been involved in a liaison with Ellie Hammond, a member of the American field crew.

"It appears that Don had a girlfriend, she is here now. She is part of the American field crew," said Esther.

"Then I guess you should have a word with her," replied Daniel.

"I intend to do that right now. You do realise that if Don is still alive, following his stunt with the maids he is almost certainly a murderer. Did you know that he made repeated requests asking us to help his seriously ill daughter? I believe that is what motivated him."

"Did we try and help?"

"America advised that there was nothing that they could do. The treatment that he was seeking is highly experimental and dangerous. His request was declined."

"A desperate father, trying to save his daughter's life?" said Daniel quizzically.

"But to murder someone in the process? It's no excuse," replied Esther with a look of disdain.

Esther noticed that Daniel had a distant look in his eyes.

"You've been to see Michaela, haven't you?"

"Yes. Just checking on her."

103

"Why do you keep going? If there is any change the hospital will let us know."

"I just feel that I should. It helps just talking to her."

"Daniel what happened is not your fault. She was warned to keep away from that book. She stole your keys. For God's sake she almost killed you. She almost killed me."

"It wasn't her. It wasn't her fault."

"Daniel, I like Michaela and I feel bad but I'm sure that the minute she comes out of the coma or if there is any change the hospital will let us know."

"I know, you're right."

Esther was genuinely concerned for Michaela but secretly hoped that she would never wake up.

***

Michaela was one of the most enthusiastic members of IES that Esther had ever met. A brilliant anthropologist with a real passion for her work. Michaela was always full of energy, which sometimes became annoying and she had absolutely no patience. Michaela oversaw the excavation at Canary Wharf and had retrieved a number of items, many of which would be later donated to the Docklands Museum. Daniel had decided that the book was to be locked away and only studied under his direct supervision. Despite all Michaela's protests Daniel would not allow the book to be studied until he had returned from the conference meeting, which he was attending with Esther. It was to discuss the building of the new Centre in Greenwich. Esther and Daniel left on the Friday unaware that Michaela had stolen his safe key.

***

Esther recalled that awful day when they returned from the meeting and she witnessed for the first time the awesome power of the book.

It was Sunday evening and Esther and Daniel walked into Daniel's office. Michaela was slumped across the desk lying on top of the open book. All over the desk were A4 pages full of handwriting in a language Daniel immediately recognised. Daniel rushed over to her and touched her shoulder. Michaela bolted upright turned and stared into his eyes.

"Michaela! Are you alright?"

There was no response. Michaela just continued to stare into his eyes. Daniel looked at the papers spread all over the desk and turned to Esther.

"This is bad Esther. This is very, very bad."

"Shall I call for an ambulance?"

"Yes. Let's get her to hospital and get her checked out."

Esther walked towards the telephone but before she could reach it a force lifted her from the ground and threw her across the room towards the door. Daniel started to make his way towards Esther to help her up but found that he could not move.

"You betray me. You betray me." said Michaela as she stood up and slowly walked towards Daniel.

"Michaela! Wake up! This is not you speaking. Don't think of the symbols just look at me."

Michaela stood still and raised her right arm. As she did so Daniel began to levitate, and he was soon pinned against the ceiling. Michaela then also began to levitate and still she stared into Daniels eyes.

"You betray me."

Daniel was by now unable to speak, the force that was pushing him against the ceiling was so powerful.

Esther got to her feet with the intention to run over to Michaela but was again thrown back. Objects within the room now began to fly through the air. Books, chairs, boxes and many other items were now hurtling around the room. Even Esther felt herself being pulled and only avoided becoming another hurtling object by hanging on to the post by the door. Michaela still staring deep into Daniel's eyes rose up closer to him.

"I can see your mind. I can see more of them. I can see thousands of them. Beautiful."

Daniel felt Michaela mentally inside his head looking at all the symbols on the black stones of his home world.

Esther by now was holding on to the post almost horizontally as the force pulled at her. She could see her handbag spinning around the room and with one hand tried to catch it as it passed.

Michaela stared at Daniel and a frown appeared on her face.

"I know who you are. I know what you are. I will show the world what you are."

Michaela held out her hand and Daniel's chain ripped from his neck and flew into her hand.

Out of the corner of her eye Esther noticed her handbag coming her way, reached out and made a desperate grab for it. Finally, she caught hold of the strap. She managed to pull herself up closer to the pillar so that she could wrap her arms round it and open the bag. Reaching inside she produced a taser gun. Holding it firmly in her hand she aimed it at Michaela. The barbs hit Michaela in the back, and she screamed in pain. Michaela fell to the floor stunned, dropping Daniel's chain as she did so, everything in the room, including Daniel also fell to the floor. Esther reached out and grabbed Daniel's chain from the floor, picked it up and ran over to him.

"Are you ok?" asked Esther, handing Daniel his chain. Esther still held the taser gun in her hand.

"I'm, fine."

Daniel got up and they both walked over to Michaela who was now lying on the floor still unconscious. The wire was still attached to her back.

"Esther, get one of our medical teams up here now!"

Esther made a call and within ten minutes the team were there. The team agreed there were no significant injuries but despite their best efforts they could not wake her, though she was not dead.

Esther looked at the handwritten papers on the desk.

"What is this? Some strange language, I recognise some letters. Arvada nestom inca......."

"No! Stop!"

"What?"

"That is the language of the Shey Atar. Somehow Michaela has been able to translate the symbols. By speaking or even thinking the words you enable the power of that symbol."

"Like a spell?"

"If you like. But how? Someone must have helped her."

Michaela was taken into medical care and there she remains, alive but still in a comatose state.

***

"I know that despite everything you still worry about her," said Esther as she gave Daniel a hug then asked Ranger Control to arrange an escort for Ellie to one of the exhibition meeting rooms where she and Aidan would be waiting.

"Sit down please." said Esther.

"What is this all about?" asked Ellie as she took a seat.

"I understand that you have a relationship with Ranger Don Magarde?" said Esther, the tone of her voice getting higher towards the end of the sentence.

"I had a relationship with Don yes. But you must know that Don is dead." Ellie replied with a confused look.

"We have evidence that he is actually alive. And not only responsible for the murder of a fellow Ranger, but also for the attempted abduction of our Ambassador." replied Esther, staring intensely at Ellie, watching for a guilty reaction.

"No, you must have it wrong. Don would not do anything like that. In any event he was killed in the maids' enclosure. The American IES informed us. His parents are devastated, as is his daughter. You do know that she is dying?" Ellie replied, becoming visibly upset.

"Have you had any contact with Don since his alleged death?" asked Esther.

"No of course not, as far as I know he is dead. I saw the grief and suffering etched on his parents' and daughter's faces. He would not do this to them, he would not do this to his daughter. You must be wrong." Ellie said with anger in her voice.

"Not even to give his daughter a chance at treatment that he believed may save her life?" asked Esther.

Ellie thought about what Esther said for a few moments then shaking her head she replied.

"Oh Don. What have you done?"

"I require you to hand over all your electronic devices including your mobile phone. Our technical support branch will interrogate them to ensure that you have not been in contact with Don. If I discover that you have been lying to me, I will ensure that you spend a long time in prison." said Esther. Her tone was one of cold indifference that sent a shudder down Ellie's spine.

"I will give you everything that you want. I think this may be partly my fault."

"Why do you think that?"

"You see once Don had completed his probation we often spoke openly about work. That is permitted so I didn't think

108

anything of it. I told him about the experiment which resulted in producing oil from water. I also told him about the book in England. I had no idea that he would do something like this I swear." As she spoke the truth dawned on her that Esther was probably correct.

"If Don makes any attempt to contact you then you must inform me immediately," said Esther.

"I will. Have you told his family?" asked Ellie.

"No, and you will not tell them either. In the meantime, you will be detained by the Rangers until I am completely satisfied that you knew nothing of this," said Esther as she turned to leave.

Esther asked Aidan to seize all Ellie's electronic devices and pass them to Kevin in order that his staff could interrogate their contents. She then returned to Daniel and updated him on the interview. They both agreed that Don had probably found a buyer for the symbols that created the oil and maybe even for the book itself. Esther again asked Daniel to cancel his plan to display the book at the exhibition. Daniel insisted that it must be shown and that the scheduled experiments would go ahead. He did however agree to increase Ranger protection for the transfer of the book to the private area in the Exhibition Centre. Once there and in its private cabinet it would take a small army to gain access to it.

Chapter 17

As the second day of the exhibition dawned DI Burns, DS Carter, Carla and Melanie made their way to the Exhibition Centre. Each had a different expectation as to what the day was going to bring. DI Burns was eagerly anticipating what the botanical displays had to offer in comparison to the research that he had been involved in during his university days. DS Carter was glad of a day away from the office, particularly today, as he had arranged to go to Soho for dinner with friends. His role tended to involve long days and today was an opportunity to finish work on time. He announced that he would be leaving at four o'clock no matter what, whilst he grinned enthusiastically.

Carla was looking forward to seeing Daniel, she had thought about him a lot since they last met. Melanie said that she didn't really care too much about the exhibition but would go along with them anyway. The girls looked at one another as Carla rolled her eyes. The four had taken public transport together and on their arrival were disappointed to see the long admission queues. They approached the first security check point and were pleasantly surprised when they were taken to one side by one of the security personnel and informed that they would be escorted personally into the Exhibition Centre via the VIP entrance. Once inside, Daniel was waiting to meet them.

"Welcome my friends," he said, extending his hand as he shook hands one by one.

"Hello Daniel. Thanks for the VIP entrance. I expected to be queuing for hours," said DI Burns.

"This is really popular. There must be hundreds of people out there. I am very much looking forward to the botanical section, I hope that it is not too busy?"

"I can think of better things to do than queue up to see a bunch of plants," said Melanie, in a disinterested tone.

"Look at it this way Mel, you could be early turn van driver instead," said Carla as she gave Melanie a dismissive look. Melanie just shrugged her shoulders.

"I think you will be surprised at what we are going to show you, but first how about we grab a coffee from the restaurant and then I will introduce you to some key people in the Centre."

"Not Esther I hope." said DI Burns, smiling.

Daniel smiled back and led the way to the VIP area of the restaurant. They selected their complimentary coffees and made their way to a table where Sonia and Oliver were already seated. Daniel introduced everyone and explained the roles that Oliver and Sonia performed. He told the officers that they would be given personal tours of the Centre but first he needed to explain a few things.

Finally! Melanie thought to herself.

They could hardly believe what they were being told as Daniel related the story and explained why the work that they were doing was so vital. He was at pains to emphasise the importance of keeping everything that they were about to learn confidential.

"Is this some kind of joke?" asked Melanie, simultaneously displaying a look of annoyance and disbelief.

"This is deadly serious. The Shey Atar have given humans a second chance but if you fail, they will destroy you. I'm sorry but that's just the way it is," replied Daniel.

"So, what's your story? I understand the Shey Atar, and I'm guessing that lady at the hospital was Shey Atar, but what about you?" asked Carla.

"We are called the Bascute. Our role is Ambassador. We each serve and protect our own Shey Atar. Carla you have seen me in my original form, the form I was created in. The Shey Atar allow us to change and the symbols that I wear allow me to hold my shape."

"But where did you all come from?" asked DS Carter.

"the Shey Atar tell us that we came to be," replied Daniel.

"And I thought this was going to be boring." said Melanie, who by now had perked up.

"I will leave you with Oliver and Sonia who will show you around the public areas and I will then join you again before we move into the private area. I hope you enjoy yourselves," said Daniel as he got up from his chair.

Daniel made his way to the Ranger control centre where he met Esther and Aidan. They had been monitoring events and all was going well, the public area was a huge success especially the AI simulation areas. The public were able to create their own environment, then monitor the direct effect that it had on the areas that they had selected to change. The smallest adjustments to the simulated land areas had the most remarkable effects. Some created lush forests or tropical jungles others were left with dried up deserts.

"How are your friends doing?" Esther asked Daniel.

"I explained what we do and why. They all took it quite well actually. DI Burns studied botanicals at university, he couldn't wait to get into the exhibit area."

"I have released Ellie; she is back in her office with her colleagues. She will not disclose anything. Kevin interrogated all devices and as far as we can tell she has made no attempt to contact Don, nor has he contacted her since his apparent death. I don't think she knows anything about this. I suppose you were right about the book's safety. I really thought they would make their move when it was most vulnerable during transfer, but nothing."

"Maybe it was the increased security measures that put them off. It is a shame I was hoping that it would draw them out. Well at least it's safe now."

"They may still attempt something when we move it back tomorrow. I will increase security again. If there is to be an attempt on the book, they will need to make it soon," said Esther.

"What makes you think that?"

"I think that, because unfortunately his daughter does not have much time left to live. I have arranged for the doctor in Switzerland to be flown over to assess her. I have ensured that his parents, and all the staff in the hospital are aware of the situation. I don't hold out much hope. Our people have assessed his theories and they do not have much confidence. I just hope it isn't too late, and that Don hears about this and calls a halt to whatever his crazy plan is." she replied.

DI Burns was fascinated by the displays of the rare and exotic plants. It took him back to his university days, as he recalled to himself how he would spend hours in the laboratory working with plant extracts attempting to create new methods of fighting crop disease. Although this was his passion at university, real life directed him into the Police. Laboratory technicians in his field unfortunately did not get paid that well, and when his wife was expecting their first child, he ended up following in his father's footsteps and he joined the Metropolitan Police. He had no regrets, he loved his job, but right now he was having a great time listening to Oliver.

DS Carter, Carla and Melanie were watching the AI simulation terminals. Sonia had calibrated the system and set it to the emergence of life. The settings enabled the conditions of the environment to be altered to see what life developed. Naturally, the passing of time had been speeded up considerably and it was fun to see what evolved. Melanie had created some green slime and long brown worms that lived on both land and water. Carla faired a little better developing grass and small unidentified insects. All was going well until she made an environment change and the simulation ended with the word Extinction flashing in red letters on the screen. "It all looks a bit like black magic to me, my nan would not approve," said Simon. "I will give the playing around a miss and just watch you two."

The three of them spent a couple of hours walking around looking at the exhibits, to Melanie's surprise she found that it had been interesting and fun. When they regrouped Sonia suggested that they made their way to the private areas. DI Burns and Oliver had already arranged to view a botanical AI simulation. Oliver said that he and the DI would catch up with the rest later, as he was sure that they were about to create a super plant antibiotic which would wipe out all plant diseases on the Earth. What DI Burns did not realise at the time but would discover a little later was that their creation would have actually wiped out all forms of plant life. Sonia, Simon, Melanie and Carla headed to the airlock door system that led into the private area and Sonia called over the radio for Daniel to join them there. They stood at the entrance to the area waiting for Daniel to reply, it was guarded by a Ranger to ensure only those authorised could enter.

"Hello," said Melanie to the guard.

He did not respond or even look at her.

"Don't say much does he?" Melanie said to Sonia.

"No. They are all like that. They take their jobs very seriously. Anyone trying to get in here without authorisation would soon know about it though." Sonia replied.

Sonia pressed the keypad and the first set of doors slid open. They walked in and the doors closed behind them. As they walked along the corridor towards the next set of doors Melanie looked at Carla and Simon.

"That was odd back there," said Melanie.

"What was?" asked Simon, his interest level raised.

"The Ranger. In the first area they were all so immaculately dressed and wearing the same uniform. That one was wearing a creased uniform and wore black shoes. The other Rangers all had dark grey boots."

"Maybe he was running late for work," said Carla sympathetically.

"So, what's so special in here?" Melanie asked Sonia.

"Well how about a plant that grows gold and silver?" replied Sonia with a smile.

"No way! See Melanie, I told you this would be fun," said Carla.

Melanie looked at Carla and raised one eyebrow.

"Oh, lighten up, maybe we will get some free gold or silver. Anyway, I know what you came here to see. And it was not a plant that grows precious metals."

"I really have no idea what you mean," said Carla, dismissively.

"I was wondering, when he is ill, does he go to a doctor or a vet?" whispered Melanie, trying to keep a straight face.

"That is a horrible thing to say. I think. In fact, I'm not sure if it is but it sounds horrible anyway." Carla replied.

Sonia pressed her fingers on another entry pad. The doors slid open and they entered the private area.

Daniel called Sonia on the radio, telling them to go ahead and that he would join them later. In the control room Esther and Daniel watched the CCTV screens that covered every area of the Centre. Esther noticed Sonia, Simon, Melanie and Carla enter the private area. It was not as crowded as the public area, containing about eighty scientists and field crews. The exhibits were around most of the room and to their left was a large laboratory with a large circular stand. On the stand lay a large round stone and above that a metal rod with an orb on the end. On the wall was a large computer monitor. There were many smaller computer screens and electrical cabinets around the room, in fact the laboratory contained a room within a room. In the wall of the area that contained the stone there was a door which led to the outer area. All the doors and panels were glass so that you could see everything in both rooms.

"Three of your friends have entered the private area," Esther said to Daniel nodding towards one of the screens.

"It looks like they are just in time for one of Jim's attempts," he replied.

Sonia told the three of them that they may find the experiment, which was about to take place interesting, and led them over to the circular laboratory. On the outside of the glass wall, scientists had gathered to observe what was about to happen on the other side of the glass.

They entered the laboratory which had five technicians, three were positioned at computer terminals, two others were in the inner room talking and examining the stone. Sonia explained that the elder of the two men was Professor Jim Buckland, he was senior IES researcher, specialising in symbol controlled atomic restructuring. The man that he was speaking with was his senior assistant, Brandon Stone. Carla and Melanie looked at each other then back at Sonia, neither had a clue what she was talking about.

Simon looked around the complex curiously as he absorbed his surroundings. Sonia, sensing that the girls were sceptical told them to watch what happened and all would become clear. Jim walked over and Sonia introduced their three guests. He was obviously excited and told them that he really thought this one was going to work. Sonia looked at them with a knowing smile.

"Good Morning CCRESI." said Jim, as he looked at the large computer monitor on the wall. CCRESI was short for Computer Controlled Radiation Eliminating Symbol Initiator.

"Good Morning Professor." CCRESI replied in an upper-class female voice.

"CCRESI please load programme Delta Mike 431," said Jim as he walked into the inner room.

"Loading Delta Mike 431. Programme loaded." CCRESI replied.

Jim then called out some instructions to the technicians as he examined the stone. It was held in place by four grips and was directly above a large piece of metal which appeared to be gold.

"CCRESI initiate programme please."

"Initiating programme. Awaiting algorithm codes."

"Jim I can type the codes in for you if you wish. You can then watch the process from the start. Maybe you will spot what's been going wrong," offered Brandon.

"Brandon I've told you before. Only I know these codes, it is far safer that way," he replied abruptly, as he typed in the code.

"Acknowledged. Delta Mike 431 symbols selected. Symbol transfer in T minus 10, 9, 8, 7, 6, 5, 4, 3, 2, 1. Symbol transfer in process."

The assembled crowd watched as the three symbols which had appeared on the computer screen were copied onto the stone by a laser beam being emitted from the orb above it.

Jim watched every action intensely, occasionally calling out an instruction to a technician.

"Symbol transfer complete. Activating phase shield in T minus 3, 2, 1. Phase shield active."

A transparent silver coloured field of energy enveloped the stone and symbols.

"Hydrogen injection is commencing. Hydrogen flow is stable. Please evacuate inner chamber before chamber lockdown. Please evacuate inner chamber before lockdown," ordered CCRESI.

Jim left the inner chamber and walked over to Brandon. They both stood watching the stone in the inner chamber.

"Evacuation detected. Inner chamber lockdown commencing. Lock down complete. Phase shift will commence in T minus 5, 4, 3, 2, 1. Phase shift activated. Shift At 20%. Shift at 60%. Shift at 80%. Phase shift complete. Commencing phase stability check. Phase shift is stable. Removing Ley-line shielding in T minus 5, 4, 3, 2, 1."

The assembled audience watched as the large gold metal slab from under the stone retracted. Once fully withdrawn the symbols began to glow gold, and they could hear a humming sound which appeared to be coming from the stone itself. Sonia explained that what they had done is move the stone and the symbols out of phase with our space time, that way should anything go wrong it would not cause any damage here. Melanie and Carla looked at each other again both still had no idea what was happening. Simon continued to look around watching the room and the assembled guests.

"The symbols are beautiful," said Melanie.

"Don't stare too much at them. You don't want to get them imprinted in your head," replied Sonia.

CCRESI continued. "Symbols fully activated. Monitoring atomic restructuring. Atomic restructuring has commenced and is at 5%. Restructuring at 30% element is stable. Restructuring at 40% radiation at 20%. Commencing radiation neutralisation. Radiation levels at 0%."

The crowd continued to watch, fascinated as the dome over the stones began to glow white and they could hear the humming getting louder. The girls then walked over to where Jim was standing and stared at the stone. Jim explained that the restructuring was taking place and that it had taken over 100 simulations with CCRESI to select the symbols that they were now using.

"Restructuring at 95%. Restructuring at 100%. Phase remains stable. Element analysis commencing." CCRESI continued.

"Please remain stable." Jim thought to himself. After a few minutes CCRESI responded.

"Element is stable. Awaiting authorisation to reverse phase shift."

As the white glow began to disappear, they could now see that something had appeared on the stone.

"It's just a piece of black rock," said Melanie.

Jim gave her a dismissive look and turned to the computer screen. He called out an authorisation code to CCRESI.

"Code accepted. Phase reversal in progress. Reversal at 20%. Reversal at 60%. Element remains stable. Phase reversal complete. Ley-line shielding activated. Phase shield deactivated. Inner chamber door unlocked. Programme Delta Mike 431 complete."

The gold bar slid back under the stone and as it disappeared the symbols stopped glowing. The silver coloured field then vanished, and they heard the inner chamber door unlock and watched the door open.

Jim was visibly excited and rushed into the inner chamber with Brandon. They appeared to be fascinated by the piece of black rock. Jim called to CCRESI to activate the element analysis laser. A red laser beam scanned the rock. They could see hundreds of lines of data appearing on the CCRESI computer monitor. Carla and Melanie both looked at Sonia waiting for an explanation as to what all the fuss was about for just a small piece of black rock. Sonia was about to speak when CCRESI burst back into life.

"Warning! Warning! Element instability detected at .01%. Warning! Warning! Element instability at 5%. Evacuate Inner chamber."

Jim and Brandon ran from the inner chamber and the door shut and locked behind them. Jim was shaking his head. "Not again." Everyone watched the rock as it began to vibrate. Red alarm lights began to flash in the laboratory and sirens sounded.

"Warning! Element instability at 35%. Phase shield activated. Phase shift commencing in T minus 5, 4, 3, 2, 1. Warning! Element instability at 75%." The rock was by now vibrating faster and faster and glowing deep red.

CCRESI then continued, "Phase shift complete. Commencing phase stability check. Warning! Element instability at 97%. Nuclear energy release imminent. Phase shift is stable."

"Nuclear energy release?" Melanie asked Sonia in disbelief.

"It's ok. It will not affect us." Sonia replied reassuringly.

They watched as the area inside the shield which contained the rock turned to a bright white light which remained for about four to five seconds. As the light faded, they could see that the black rock was gone, the stone was bare.

"Energy release complete. Scanning for Element. No element found. Scanning for residue. No residue found. Radiation neutralisation in progress. Neutralisation complete radiation at 0%. Calculating energy and temperature release. Calculating.......
Calculating........."

Jim and his technicians waited as CCRESI continued making calculations. It was still calculating 5 minutes later when suddenly it responded.

"Calculations complete. Results displayed."

The two women looked at the large numbers in kelvin and terra joules which meant nothing to them. Jim walked over to Melanie.

"That piece of rock you mentioned just created the equivalent energy of one thousand hydrogen bombs," he said as he walked towards a technician shouting.

"Come on boys and girls. You all know the routine let's get started on the data that CCRESI collected. Let's see if we can find out what went wrong this time."

"You are playing with hydrogen bombs in London." Melanie said to Sonia with a look of disbelief.

Sonia explained that they were perfectly safe, and that the computer would detect any danger, as it had just demonstrated, and then phase the element out of our space time. Sonia explained that Jim had in fact created dark matter, and that if they could just stabilise it, the world would have a limitless supply of clean energy.

Following the experiment Simon walked back over and met up with the girls. "I don't like something here," he said. "Not the experiments, just something in my water gives me a funny feeling about this place. I can't quite put my finger on it. Anyway, it is just coming up to four o'clock and I am off. Tell the guvnor I will be in at eight in the morning. See you all." With that Simon left. Sonia continued the tour of the private area, Carla and Melanie were amazed at what they saw. They had never seen such exotic creatures and striking plant life. Melanie asked if she could have one of their gold and silver plants, Sonia politely declined her request laughing. Carla couldn't understand why among all these strange exhibits China had supplied a small black spider, around four inches in diameter. What was so special about that? she asked. Sonia said she would leave the Chinese expert to explain the significance of the Chinese Tree Spider. They spent many more hours viewing the exhibits and listening to the scientists explain what they were hoping to achieve with each one. No-one ventured too close to the maid display, everyone stood way back as the sight just filled them with an unknown fear.

Chapter 18

Don was struggling with Daniel and a doorman outside Heels Bar when he saw the Police vehicle appear in the distance. He could not believe they had turned up, especially as he was so close to forcing Daniel into the bar. Once they arrived and Daniel had swung the punch and been arrested Don melted away into the night and the doorman disappeared back inside the bar. The Bulgarian had already arranged for Daniel to be taken by boat through a rear entrance to a secure location that Don was unaware of. He knew that The Bulgarian's people in the club would let him know that the kidnap bid had failed and that he would be extremely unimpressed. The drug that had been slipped into Daniel's drink was supposed to make him compliant. Daniel's sudden truculence had surprised him as it had seemed to work in the restaurant, Don was wearing a Ranger uniform under his coat and after allowing a few minutes for the drugged coffee to take effect he removed his outer coat and approached Daniel. Daniel had initially become drowsy and when informed by Don that he had an urgent meeting that he needed to attend Daniel followed him willingly to the waiting car. For most of the journey to the club Daniel appeared drowsy and co-operative, however when they arrived his demeanour changed. He became reluctant to comply with the instructions to go into the club and although both Don and the doorman tried, they failed to persuade him. The drug had made him incredibly strong, at one point lifting the huge doorman completely off his feet. The plan had failed and now Don had to face The Bulgarian. The idea to abduct Daniel alone, wearing one of his old uniforms was his. He would now be lucky if The Bulgarian did not order his murder. He was also aware that IES suspicions would be raised and they would investigate the incident thoroughly. The Bulgarian had already made it perfectly clear that he wanted no one poking into his affairs, and that this plan had better not draw attention to him. Don however had something that he could bargain with. Something that The Bulgarian did not know about. Don knew the layout of the complex; he knew the location of the pod and most importantly of all he knew where the book would be and when it would be there. They no longer needed Daniel; they could obtain the book themselves. The Bulgarian punished failure most severely and Don had received a painful and permanent reminder, only his fitness had saved his life. The Bulgarian had considered his new idea but this time some of his top people would go along and he would make the arrangements. He told him, that if he failed again both he and his daughter would die. As much as Don now regretted what he had done there was no going back.

***

Esther and Daniel remained in the Ranger control room monitoring the Centre activities on the CCTV screens. The exhibition appeared to be a success and all the visitors seemed to be enjoying themselves. In common with all the other worldwide IES visitor centres they were working towards one of their Shey Atar targets, to change the habits of the world's population and clean up the mess that people had made of the environment. Daniel was about to make his way to the private area to meet with Sonia, as he had seen that Oliver and Matt were still looking around the public area exhibits. Matt seemed very happy at the way events had worked out.

Suddenly Kevin rushed into to the control room and made his way straight over to them both.

"I have some news!"

"What's wrong Kevin?" asked Esther.

"You know I checked all Ellie's devices and we found nothing?"

"Don't tell me you missed something?"

"No. There was nothing on them we thoroughly checked them all. But then I considered interrogating her remote access to the server in the US. That revealed that someone has been logging into her account and reading her emails. It had been very cleverly hidden, bouncing the login off several proxy servers but it was there."

"So, assuming this is Don, and he has somehow managed to get Ellie's password what does he know?"

"I viewed every page that he had opened. He read all emails about this visit. He also opened the documentation showing the blueprint for the maid transfer pod."

"Well the pod docked fine and we had no incidents," said Daniel.

"It gets worse. The lay-out and blueprints of the Exhibition Centre's private area where the pod would dock were e-mailed to Ellie. He downloaded them."

"I was expecting him to go for the book during transfer. He didn't. He is going to attack us from the river. I predict that he will break directly into the private area. Have we seen anything odd on the cameras?" Esther asked the control room Rangers.

"We had a little static on some of them a short time ago, but apart from that nothing," replied one of the Rangers.

"Has anything approached the Centre from the river during the last week?"

"Nothing reported. To double check we would need to play back the recordings in real time, that will take the equivalent of the whole week, depending on how many viewers we utilise."

"Get Aidan up here immediately please. We need that CCTV checked and I want the security of the entire riverside exterior of the Centre reviewed."

Chapter 19

On the evening of the opening day of the exhibition a Sunseeker yacht pulled into Greenwich Reach and moored up. Don was aboard the vessel with the team that The Bulgarian had insisted accompany him. Events had been stepped up considerably since Don explained what the book was capable of. The whole event was now more serious than Don could ever have originally imagined. He knew that the only reason for him still being alive was his intimate knowledge of IES. How he wished that he could call a halt to the crime that he was intrinsically involved in. All that it would take was for him to contact someone in IES and warn them, but he knew that was impossible. He had been a virtual prisoner since the failure to abduct Daniel and he had made no outside contact with anyone. Any attempt by him to try to warn someone would result in his immediate death. Even if he did escape, they would kill Corin.

Once the yacht was moored an underwater drone with a tether was lowered into the water and remotely navigated to the underside of the Exhibition Centre. The drone attached the cable to the underwater supports and was then recalled to the yacht. At nightfall once the Centre was closed, Don and his accomplices slipped into the cold dark river. The operation leader was a female Iraqi sociopath Dr. Kaya Kouri. They were all wearing full scuba diving kit; however, the water was still very cold, very dark, visibility was almost zero and they had to feel their way by slowly pulling themselves along the rope that the drone had earlier attached. Once they reached the end of the rope, they knew that they were underneath the structure. They surfaced and climbed a maintenance ladder to a lower deck. The decks were shown on the blueprint that Don had supplied and were used by maintenance staff. It had also been used by the US field crew to ensure the pod was perfectly connected to the Centre. They each removed their diving equipment and placed it into a large bag that they had brought with them. The bag was lowered into the water from where the drone which had been following them towed it back to the yacht. Don sat on the deck with the others waiting to be given the signal to move. The plan was to stay there and wait until the Centre was busy and then slip in unnoticed through the service corridor entrance.

Don lay down and made himself as comfortable as he could. A sadness came over him as he thought of his beautiful Corin. He had a feeling that he would never see her again. As he looked around, he realised that he was amongst a group of obviously hardened men. He could hear that they spoke in Eastern European or Russian accents and two of the group were dressed in Rangers uniforms that had been supplied by The Bulgarian. The only noticeable difference was their footwear. They were forced to wear the flat black shoes that they brought with them as the boots were too cumbersome for the underwater section of the operation. The other three men wore casual shirt and trousers with white coats over the top and Russian IES field crew identity badges pinned to the lapels, all carried weapons under the coats. Don was wearing one of his old Ranger uniforms but was not given a weapon as Kaya had already made it perfectly clear that she did not trust him. She was also the person responsible for the large scar that Don bore on his back. Her mother was previously one of Saddam Hussein's personal female bodyguards. She had instilled in her that she needed to fight hard for what she wanted and to keep what she already had. Her mother protected Saddam, killing many of his enemies but when the invasion took place in 2003, all was obviously lost so she made plans to escape from the country. Along with her daughter Kaya, and a trusted soldier colleague they made their way to a pre-arranged meeting point. From there they were transported to a nondescript flat inside which over a period of time she had stored a considerable quantity of valuables, ready for onward movement out of the country should it be necessary. The group were almost at the border when a sniper bullet hit her mother in the back paralysing her. Both the soldier and Kaya realised that due to the extent of her injury it would be difficult to smuggle her out of the country. There was a real danger that if she were captured, she would subsequently be tortured and may reveal their plans. The soldier drew his weapon intending to kill her, but Kaya stepped in and took the gun from him. Kaya then turned and shot her mother in the head. Leaving her mother's lifeless body where she fell the two remaining fugitives fled.

In the ensuing chaos they both managed to escape from Iraq and travelled through many countries. Eventually they settled in the Bulgarian capital Sofia. After changing her name, she completed her studies and eventually enrolled into medical school. After many years she qualified as a surgeon and went on to establish a private clinic which catered for the very wealthy. Dr Kaya Kouri, a particularly unpleasant individual provided a specialist service combining both her work and her hobby. Using an organised crime network, she acquired her victims, they were usually homeless people, or from vulnerable groups where their disappearance would not be noticed. She then removed their organs and sold them on for use in transplants. She took great pride in removing them from the victim personally, often whilst they were still conscious. She was also a member of The

Bulgarian's personal protection team, a crack squad of ruthless criminals.

Kaya roused the team; it was time to enter the next phase of the operation. They cautiously climbed the access ladder. The entrance to the exhibition was behind the South American display and as there were quite a few people already in the exhibit area they individually entered the Centre unnoticed. The disguised Rangers immediately made their way to the Ranger standing on guard at the exit door followed by Kaya. As they approached him, they smiled and moved in close. Pressing his concealed weapon into the guard's ribs one of the Rangers told him to follow him and if he made any attempt to raise the alarm, he would shoot him dead. Don watched as the helpless Ranger walked past him, a feeling of guilt and betrayal came over him. He knew that he was lucky to have survived this far as Kaya had pressed for his execution following the mess up with the failed abduction. Fortunately, his friend Tom must have had some influence with The Bulgarian because, despite Kaya's insistence on killing him, The Bulgarian had promised to keep to his word, as long as Don delivered. How he now wished he had never started this whole thing.

They took the guard back to the service corridor from where they entered and he was tied up and gagged, while the impostor Ranger remained at the exit door. Kaya injected him with a serum and the guard fell unconscious, the impostor guard and Kaya returned to join their colleague. As they approached the access door for no apparent reason the door opened. Kaya and one of the Rangers entered the entrance tunnel and walked towards the entrance door. Kaya lay down on the floor and her colleague swiped his card to open the door. He called for the Ranger outside to come and help with the lady collapsed on the floor and without a second thought the Ranger rushed in. Kaya jumped up pointing a gun at him. The impostor Ranger took his place, he would alert them if anything suspicious was occurring outside. Kaya led the prisoner to the service corridor followed by one of her team. There he was also tied and drugged. All they now had to do was mix with the crowd and wait to watch the experiment, they had to be certain that it worked before acting. Kaya walked over to Don.

"If this is all bullshit, I will personally dissect you," she said with a smile.

"You've seen my notes. It will work," replied Don, hoping that he was right.

"Well at least your camera jamming device seems to have worked. I imagine we will be spotted soon enough so let's hope everything else that you have designed works."

The impostors now just waited, avoiding any direct contact with the others in the Centre and communicating via the radio earpieces and microphones that they were discreetly wearing.

The visitors in the Centre all began moving towards the laboratory area, standing around it and watching intently through the glass panels. The entrance door opened and in walked Sonia, Carla and Melanie, who also made their way to the laboratory area. As everyone intently watched the experiment nobody noticed as Kaya ordered two of her team, who were carrying backpacks, over to the fire exits.

Chapter 20

Aidan entered the control room and walked across to where Esther and Daniel were speaking. Esther summarised the situation, explaining her theory of a riverside attack. Aidan sat down at a CCTV terminal and began examining the screens, he panned the cameras around, scanning the Centre and its occupants. Aidan looked intently in Esther's direction.

"I'm afraid your attack has already started."

"What do you mean?"

"The Ranger at both the entrance and inside are not my staff. I played back some CCTV footage and both my Rangers have been taken out into the access areas. I can also see three males and a female wearing incorrect ID passes and not only that, Don Magarde is amongst them," he said zooming the camera onto Don's face.

"What do we do?" asked Daniel.

"We have to assume that they are armed so we can't just go rushing in. They have plenty of hostages if they need them but at the moment they just seem to be observing. Esther, do you want us to start discreetly evacuating the public areas?" asked Aidan.

"No, they could have people watching the Centre from the outside. Aidan get our air and marine support on standby. They must come out eventually and let's ensure that no one attempts to enter the private area. Do it discreetly, we don't want to spook the person on the door."

"Okay. We will use a different encrypted channel; they are bound to be listening in on the radios they will have taken from our Rangers."

"I need to speak to Don. I need to try and talk him out of this. The problem is that I will make them aware that we know they are in there," said Esther.

"I will call the laboratory and speak to Jim. I can brief him on what is happening, maybe he can provide us with some sort of an update. I have to admit though, I suspect they knew that we would quickly spot them," she added.

"I will secure facial images of them all and run them through the national and international security systems. Hopefully, we will get some idea of who Don is working with," offered Aidan.

***

Once the experiment was over Kaya entered the laboratory outer area and saw Professor Buckland briefly speaking with three women before crossing the room to speak to his technicians. Kaya walked towards him purposefully.

"Hello Professor Buckland," she said extending her hand.

Jim turned to face Kaya, looking at her trying to remember if they had met before.

"Hello. I'm sorry have we met?" said Jim as he shook her hand.

"No Professor we have not. My name is Doctor Kaya Kouri and I have something important that I need to discuss with you."

Kaya took Jim to one side and explained that she was in the company of several men strategically placed around the room and that any attempt to cause alarm or not cooperate would result in shootings. Kaya told him to do exactly as she instructed and make no attempt to alert anyone. Kaya's orders were that he was to collect the book then make an excuse to leave the laboratory and accompany her to the service corridor door. Jim saw that she was armed, and he did not want anyone getting hurt. Just as he was about to walk towards the book a technician approached him and told him that he had an urgent phone call from Esther.

Jim looked to Kaya, his expression asking her for permission to take the call.

"Go ahead. I knew that they would have spotted us by now," she said as she walked over to the phone with him. Jim sent the technician away and Kaya took the handset. Esther could see on the camera that she had taken hold of the telephone.

"Who is this?" asked Esther.

"It doesn't matter who I am just listen. No doubt you will have seen that I am not alone, and we are all armed. Nobody needs to get hurt or even know that we are here. We will collect what we want and leave the exhibition without anyone being harmed as long as you do exactly what I say."

"What is it that you want?"

"We are leaving here with the professor, the book, and one other hostage. As long as you comply with my orders the hostages will be returned unharmed in a few days' time. You will make no attempt to enter here or stop us as we leave. I do not want to see anyone outside when we exit the complex."

"Listen, you have no idea what forces you are dealing with here; you cannot take that book."

"Do not argue with me. If you give me a reason to do so I will kill the hostages, do not doubt me. I am going to put someone on the phone."

Kaya turned to Jim and asked who the girl was that he was speaking to earlier. Jim said that he did not know her and that she was just a visitor. Kaya told him to call her over and tell her she was wanted on the phone. Jim walked over to Melanie and Carla.

"Melanie, Esther is on the phone for you," said Jim, he was very aware that he was being closely monitored by Kaya.

"Oh God! What does she want?"

"Have you been a naughty girl?" asked Carla enquiringly.

"Of course. Always." Melanie said smiling as she walked over to the phone.

In the meantime, Don was at the entrance with the impostor Ranger when Kaya signalled him to start his part of the plan. Don opened the first door and walked to the end of the corridor. The entrance door opened and the Ranger standing outside came into the corridor. The door closed and Don opened the internal access panel. His devices would ensure that the doors were locked shut and it would be impossible to open them.

As Don was working on the internal door a technician approached asking if she could leave. He explained that they were experiencing problems with the doors and that they were currently waiting for maintenance. An announcement would be made once the doors were repaired. As she walked away Don and the two Rangers began to make their way to the service corridor exit where the other members of the team were waiting. He could see that Kaya was also heading in the same direction.

Melanie listened to what Esther had to say as she stared at Kaya. All her police and military training came to the forefront of her mind. She was focused on exactly what was happening, she knew that she was a hostage and she knew that she had to ensure that no one got hurt. Kaya told her to make her excuses to her friend and that they were leaving now. Jim picked the book, placing it in his satchel. As he did so he told his colleagues he wanted to study some new symbols in his office. They thought nothing of it as he walked away, they were all far too busy trying to establish what went wrong with the last experiment. Melanie walked over to Carla.

"What did she want?"

"Oh, nothing she just wanted to check we were having a good time."

"Really? How weird."

"Listen I just need to use the toilet; I will be right back."

"Sure, okay."

Carla watched as Melanie walked away towards the service exit.

"Hey Mel, the toilets are the other way."

Melanie ignored Carla and continued to walk towards the service door exit behind Jim and Kaya.

"Mel! Where are you going?"

Carla began to follow Melanie. Melanie turned her head toward Carla staring intently.

"Carla just go back please."

As Esther monitored the unfolding drama on CCTV, she spotted that Carla had started to follow Melanie, she knew that this would annoy Kaya and telephoned the laboratory in an attempt to lure Carla away. The call was too late, Kaya had noticed that Carla was now following and turned towards her. Taking her gun from her shoulder holster she pointed it at Carla.

"Some people just do not listen."

Don saw Kaya raise her gun and ran towards her.

"No! No shooting."

Kaya pulled the trigger and the bullet hit Don in the chest as he ran between Kaya and Carla. Don would have been dead before he hit the ground. He would never see his beautiful Corin again.

Screams and panic filled the Centre as people realised what just happened. The crowds instinctively fell to the ground taking cover where they could, Carla dropped down behind a nearby desk. That stranger had saved her life, that should have been her lying there on the floor, she thought to herself. Carla felt terrified and helpless thinking that the woman may walk over any second and shoot her. Then she heard her shout.

"Nobody move, we are leaving now. Stay exactly where you are, and nobody else will get hurt."

Kaya ordered her team and the hostages into the corridor. One of the Russians dragged the two drugged Rangers back into the Centre. The door they exited from was then shut and jammed from the outside with a metal bar so that it could not be opened. Kaya had a Rangers radio and again reminded control that she did not want to see anybody outside as she left.

Carla ran over to Don who was lying on the floor to check on his condition, he was clearly dead, and she suddenly felt a great sadness for him. He had saved her life and she didn't even know who he was. Pulling herself together she knew that she had to take charge, people were distressed, some were crying. Carla checked on the two Rangers lying on the floor. They were blearily beginning to come round. She then cautiously went over to the service corridor exit door and tried to open it. It was jammed.

Chapter 21

"Listen to me everybody. My name is Carla and I am a Police Officer. Please try and remain calm.

One of the visitors in the Centre then called out to Carla. "Excuse me Officer, I think you should see this."

Carla walked over to the man and he pointed towards the fire exit door. On the door handle was a device with wires protruding from a bundle of what was clearly explosives. On top of device was a card with 'BOOM' written on it. Carla looked over to the other fire exit and the same device was on that door too. Another lady called to Carla from the main entrance door.

"This door isn't working it won't open."

"Get away from there now. There may be a device attached to that too!" She quickly moved away.

"Okay everyone, move as far as you can away from the fire exits. It looks as if they have planted bombs on the doors. Please turn off all mobile phones, the signal may detonate the devices."

People quickly moved away from the doors deeper into the middle of the room, switching off their phones as they did so. Carla hurried over to a telephone that was ringing in the laboratory area.

"Hello."

"Carla it's Esther. We have been monitoring the CCTV."

"What the hell is going on? Who were those people and why have they taken Melanie?"

"Melanie and Jim have been taken hostage. I will explain it all later. How are you?"

"We can't get out of the fire exits because they have planted bombs on the doors. The main door will not open. I can't see a device on it but there may be one on the other side."

"Okay, one minute."

Esther had already sent Kevin and his team down to the main door to try and gain access.

"Aidan tell Kevin to stop what they are doing and get away from the door."

Aidan ran out of the control room to pass the instruction.

"Carla listen. Those people responsible have left on a boat, we are monitoring them on CCTV. We will come in from the service corridor exit and get you out that way."

At that moment there was an almighty explosion. The Centre shook and people fell to the floor, some were thrown across the room by the force of the blast. There was panic and people screaming as they ran away from the seat of the explosion. Some of the display cabinets had shifted and been damaged by the force, the toughened glass on two of them was broken, more importantly, the maids pod seal had fractured. The water from the maids pod was leaking directly into the river and the maid was thrashing around in the display unit which in turn was causing the gap to widen. Carla was momentarily stunned by the explosion and had dropped the telephone; her ears were still ringing when she picked it up again.

The CCTV monitors all showed an almighty flash, some screens went blank. Esther shouted down the phone.

"Carla! Carla! Are you okay?"

"Yes. I'm fine. What happened?"

"They must have detonated a device in the service corridor. Carla it may take us some time to free you. We need to confirm that there are no secondary devices. Try not worry I will get you all out as soon as I can."

139

"Okay. I will check on the others."

"Leave this line open on hands free. Okay?"

"Yes. I will get back to you."

Esther turned to the Rangers in the control room.

"I need the Army bomb disposal team to check the service corridor before we make any rescue attempt." As she said this Kevin and Aidan returned.

"Aidan ensure that the boat is tracked and get onto head of IES communications and explain what has happened, we need them down here to deal with the press and public. Tell them our cover story is that a fuel cell exploded.

"Shall I evacuate the public area?"

"Yes please. Explain that it is just a precaution and there is nothing to worry about. And get the Police to cordon off this area. I don't want anyone coming near this Centre."

"Anything I can do?"

"Yes Kevin, Aidan had arranged for the images of those involved from the CCTV to be checked against national and international databases to try and establish who we are dealing with. Please can you chase it up?"

Daniel watched as Esther took control of the situation, he could not help but feel concerned for Carla, he had taken quite a liking to her and he wished there was something more that he could do. He knew that the Shey Atar would never agree to open a portal and he would then be forced to explain that the book had been stolen. He was aware that although the current situation was serious it would be nothing compared to what would happen if the thieves tried to use the symbols in the book outside an agreed IES location. The Shey Atar would sense it and immediately assume that their existence had been revealed. What would follow would be Armageddon.

Carla walked over to Sonia who was helping some injured using the first aid kits as she had directed.

"How are we doing Sonia?"

"Mostly just shaken, some have minor bruises and cuts. One lady is unconscious but breathing and I cannot rouse her, I think she may be concussed. We need to get her to hospital as soon as possible."

"Okay I will let Esther know."

Carla searched around the area where the explosion had occurred. It had knocked out the power to the unit, the lights went out and the air conditioning had stopped working. The emergency power supply engaged itself and the lighting had returned. The interior wall of the Centre had buckled but it remained intact preventing any escape. Some of the display cabinets had been damaged in the explosion. The glass panels on some were cracked and the Chinese cabinet's glass was completely smashed. The maids cabinet had small cracks to the bottom but remained intact, however the exterior seal to the Centre was damaged and water was leaking into the Thames. Carla watched the maid as it smashed around in its cabinet obviously distressed by the explosion. She watched as it smashed against the glass knowing that if the glass gave way they would be stuck in the Centre with that thing on the loose. As she turned, she realised that everyone else was staring at the cabinet and she knew they were all thinking the same thing.

Carla walked back to the laboratory.

"Esther are you there? Can you hear me?"

"Yes, Carla I'm here."

"We need to get out of here now. We have an unconscious female; Sonia thinks that she may be concussed. We need to get her to hospital sooner rather than later."

"Carla the Army bomb disposal team will be with you shortly and as soon as they clear that service corridor, we will break our way in. In the meantime, just do your best for her."

"Okay, but please hurry."

Suddenly a second alarm sounded, this one a semitone higher than the first.

"Carla what's that?"

"I don't know. Wait I will check."

As Carla walked out of the laboratory one of the technicians ran up to her.

"Carla, we have just checked the Japanese cabinet. The glass is fractured. Those recent alarms are to warn of carbon monoxide. It is leaking from the cabinets."

"Can we stop it?"

"We will try and patch it up, but you must tell everyone to stand up. The gas is heavier than air so will sink to the floor, but it is deadly. You can't smell or see it but this gas from that cabinet will kill you."

"Oh great! Okay do what you can. Sonia come here please."

Sonia got up from her patient and walked over to Carla.

"Sonia a cabinet is leaking carbon monoxide. There's no ventilation in here and the air conditioning is not working. Don't panic people, but we need to get the injured off the floor and onto the tables. Identify some people to help lift that lady onto a table and explain to everyone else that they must remain standing."

"We really shouldn't move her."

"If we don't, she will die."

Sonia shook her head in disbelief as she began to organise people.

Carla made her way back to the telephone.

"Esther!"

"Yes Carla."

Carla spoke quietly into the handset; she didn't want to let the others know that she was worried.

"You need to get us out now! The maid's glass is cracked, and it is going wild. If that thing gets in here with us it will be a bloodbath. If that was not enough, a cabinet is leaking carbon monoxide and we have no ventilation or air conditioning."

"Okay. I see that you are arranging for the injured to be moved onto tables. Good. The army are on their way they will be there soon. Please hold tight Carla and don't worry. I will get you out."

"I will do my best. Oh, Esther another thing the exterior seal to the maid's cabinet is loose. It is banging around in there and if the gap becomes much wider it will potentially escape into the Thames."

"Oh fantastic, that is all we need."

Esther turned to Aidan.

"Where the hell are the Army! Aidan can you chase them up please? Someone get the American field crew out to fix that seal."

Carla walked back into the Centre where the injured were now on tables. A Chinese male walked over to her.

"Excuse me, my name is Zhang Wei, I am the Chinese representative."

"Yes."

"I need to tell you something. I know that you have a lot to deal with right now, but I thought you should know something."

"What is it?"

"The glass on my display cabinet has been broken and consequently the environmental controls are now useless. Come with me please."

143

The man walked over to his cabinet and Carla followed.

"I remember this one. It was the one with the small spider in."

"Yes, but it has now escaped."

"Is it dangerous?"

"Not really. Not yet."

"Not yet, what do you mean?"

"Now that it is out of its controlled habitat it will quickly grow. If it finds food, it will grow even quicker."

"Grow. How big potentially?"

"It will eventually grow to about six feet long. But that will take some time. I would say in a couple of hours it will be about twelve inches long."

Carla sighed. What next? We didn't cover this in the knowledge and reasoning tests at Hendon, she thought to herself.

"Please do not say anything about this to the others and see if you can discreetly try and locate it."

Carla sat on the edge of the table waiting to hear from Esther. Looking around the dimly lit room she saw the worried expressions on people's faces. Sonia and her assistants were doing their best, treating and re-assuring people. Sonia had done well but it still did not distract from the constant sound of the two alarms and the thrashing of the maid against the glass. Sonia thought about Melanie and hoped that she was okay. Looking at the body of the man on the floor, by now covered with a white coat, she wondered who he was.

A young lady standing on the table next to Carla's jumped down and walked towards Don's body which lay on the floor and stood staring at it. She turned to Carla.

"Excuse me, are you sure that he is dead?"

"Yes, I checked I'm afraid he is."

"But I'm sure I just saw the coat move."

Carla looked down at the body and she too saw the coat moving.

"Oh my god' he's still alive. Quick somebody help me get him onto a table."

Carla ran over to Don and pulled the coat off him. She recoiled and screamed at what she saw.

Chapter 22

In the meantime, Esther had left the control room as everything was in hand and she needed to speak to Ellie in order to give her the terrible news, this was something that she dreaded having to do. Esther had delivered death messages too many times in her career. It never got any easier and she thought to herself that it never should.

Aidan and his team continued to monitor the boat and completed a running log of its location every few minutes. Esther couldn't help but wonder what they were up to, they must have known that they would be monitored and that they were never going to escape. What were they up to? She thought to herself. And how would the Shey Atar react once they realised that the book had been stolen with the accompanying risk of exposure? The idea was too terrifying to contemplate, they had always insisted that their existence was kept a secret from all but IES personnel. Esther realised that unless knowledge of the theft was immediately contained it could be the beginning of the end for the human race. She explained the tragic circumstances of Don's death to Ellie and asked her to get a plane back to America in order to confirm his death to Don's parents.

Esther walked into the restaurant and sat down at the table with Professor Chambers and DI Burns. She was just about to explain the situation to them when there was another explosion. It came from the street level side of the building. All three ran out of the restaurant towards the control room.

***

Back in the Centre Carla looked down at Don's body and saw a spider as big as her hand, it was jet black and positioned on Don's chest. It was feeding around his neck, its mouth parts visible as it chewed on his flesh. She jumped back throwing the coat back over it. The spider disturbed by this commotion ran across the floor and up the wall. They all stared as it crawled up the wall and then when it was halfway up it disappeared before their eyes.

Carla turned and looked at Zhang.

"I take it that is yours?"

"Yes. He is bigger than I thought he would be by now."

"Why did it disappear?"

"It did not disappear. They can camouflage themselves. They are incredible creatures you see we use the skin and silk; they have amazing properties."

Before he could finish telling Carla his story her attention was drawn to a young lady a few tables away. She was distressed and upset.

The young lady's name was Alice Matthews an unremarkable lady, rather plain really. She never stood out in a crowd and never sought attention. Her work was her life and her passion was horticulture. Ever since she was a young girl Alice had loved plants. As a child she had her own section of the family garden where she grew vegetables and herbs for her mother. At school she studied hard and years later obtained her dream job as a botanist. She could not believe it when she was approached by IES and offered a research position. Living alone with just her pet cat for company all in her world was perfect. However, Alice had an experience as a child from which she never recovered. She woke one morning to find a spider crawling on her stomach towards her face. That arachnophobia had remained with her for her entire life and it filled her with dread to even imagine being in the same room as a spider.

Carla watched as the young lady began shouting hysterically. "I have to get out of here! I have to get out of here!" Carla could see that two people were trying to restrain Alice, she was in a darkened room with the one thing that she feared the most. All rationality left her. She had to get away, she just had to get out. Alice pulled away and began to run towards the fire exit.

"No! Stop!" Carla shouted.

Alice did not hear her. Auditory exclusion had taken over and nothing mattered except escaping from the room, away from the thing that she feared the most. She continued to run towards the fire exit.

"Everybody, get down!" shouted Carla, realising that Alice was not going to stop.

The explosion caused by her opening of the door was not as large as the first one, but it was powerful enough to blow Alice to pieces. It was no consolation, but at least they now had a way out.

Esther and the others entered the control room where they were briefed on what had just occurred. She could see on the cameras that the press, the IES representatives and the emergency services were present in the street outside. Slowly casualties began to emerge from the Centre and were escorted to the waiting ambulances. Esther made her way with Daniel and DI Burns to the fire exit from where the people were exiting the building. The IES representatives were having a hard time trying to explain the events to the press but they were sticking with the story of faulty power cells. The American field crew advised Esther that the maids pod had now been secured.

They watched as the casualties were brought out and eventually Carla appeared. Carla was looking a little dazed and as they walked over to her Esther asked how she was. Carla was covered in dust, but she said she was fine, though her concern was for Melanie. She asked if anyone had heard anything and wanted to know what was going on. Esther suggested that they all meet in the control room for a hot debrief, they needed to assess what had happened and consider which, if any, fast time actions they could take. Daniel took Carla's hand offering her a drink of water. He told her how glad he was that she was okay and how sorry he was for getting her and her friends involved in all this. Carla reassured him that he was very kind, but the only thing that she was concerned about was getting her friend back safe and unharmed.

They all made their way back into the Centre and up to the control room leaving the Army explosives experts to deal with the other devices and the emergency services to take care of the casualties. Esther asked all the uninjured staff to go to the restaurant where they would be looked after and from where transport would be arranged to get them home. IES representatives were assigned to travel with any staff that needed to go to the hospital and their brief was to update Esther on their progress and stay with them until their discharge.

In the control room were Esther, Daniel, Carla, DI Burns, Aidan, Oliver, Sonia and Kevin. Esther chaired the debrief meeting and they each in turn told her of their experience and what they had witnessed. At the conclusion Esther gave them an overview of all that had happened including the fact that the terrorist group had stolen the book and taken Jim and Melanie as hostages. She reminded them of the gravity of the situation and that if the Shey Atar believed that their existence had been exposed beyond IES the consequences were too terrible to contemplate. Aidan advised that the yacht was still being monitored and that it continued to head down the river towards the open sea. Esther said that the priority was to retrieve the book and detain those responsible as soon as possible but obviously as they had hostages that would be difficult. She told them that a Navy destroyer had been deployed to the area and that she expected to negotiate with Kaya once it was obvious that they had no escape. Aidan suggested that there must be a plan, just cruising out to sea made no sense after all the work they put into getting into the Centre. Especially taking into account their inability to outrun The Royal Navy. Esther agreed but pointed out that all they could do for now was wait and see. Carla asked if any attempt had been made to contact them to check on Melanie. Esther said that although they took a Ranger radio with them there was no reply despite repeated attempts to communicate with them. Esther asked Daniel how long it would be before the Shey Atar would realise that the book was missing, and what were they likely to do. He told them that if the book crossed a Ley line the symbols inside it would react and that the Shey Atar would realise that the book was outside the permitted IES locations. Their response would most likely be immediate, firstly contacting the Ambassadors to establish why that was occurring. Once they had confirmation that the rules had been broken, they would act as promised, they would start on the total eradication of mankind. He went on to say that they would be ruthless and there was nothing that anyone could do would stop them. Fortunately, their current direction was away from any lines but that he would update them should they get close to one.

Esther asked Oliver and Sonia to work with Kevin's team to get the Centre back up and running once the army had given the all clear, and that they would be provided with whatever resources they needed. The press line would remain the same, faulty fuel cells and Kevin was asked to assemble something that resembled a burnt fuel cell to corroborate the story. She said that

Carla and DI Burns should return home and that she would keep them updated, both refused and said they were staying until Melanie was back.

As this conversation was taking place a control room operative called them, to say that the yacht had stopped. They watched the live images being broadcast by their air unit. The yacht had left the estuary and come to a stop in the sea off the Essex coast. The Naval destroyer was in the area but out of sight of the boat. As they watched, from nowhere a submarine rose out of the sea. The transfer of staff and items from the yacht to the submarine was quick and efficient, within minutes the submarine had dived below the water line. Esther ordered the destroyer to locate and track them. Almost immediately the Navy informed her that they were finding it impossible to locate the vessel. The same response came from the air support unit, similarly from satellite tracking. They were gone.

"Well what now? How do we find Melanie?" asked Carla.

"We have no way of finding them and the moment that sub crosses a Ley line we are all finished," replied Aidan in a resigned tone.

Esther sank back into a chair with a look of defeat. She knew that she had failed and there was nothing that she could do. Suddenly realising her behaviour was affecting the morale of the others she looked up at them. She ordered Aidan to alert all IES locations, and ask them to begin searching for this submarine, also to search all databases in order to find the owner.

Kevin looked around sheepishly as he said, "I realise that my actions may have overstepped my authority, but I think that you ought to know that one of my technicians placed a tracking device on the book. I know that I should have checked first, but it just seemed like a sensible idea to me. It will not activate until the book is opened so that if scanned it will not be detected."

Esther looked up at Kevin, rose from her chair and walked over to him.

"Kevin! I could kiss you," she said, much to everyone's surprise.

A control room operator called over to Daniel informing him that they had received an incoming call for him from the Russian Ambassador. Daniel looked at the large video conference screen and the image of a man appeared.

"Hello Daniel."

"Hello Gabriel."

"Is there a problem as your Centre has been all over the news? We have been tracking some rather unusual activities, is there something we should know about?" he asked.

"It's a minor problem but we are dealing with it, nothing to worry about Gabriel."

"If there is anything that I can help with Daniel please ask. I wouldn't want anything to go wrong with the project. We have both worked so hard on this," said Gabriel implying that he knew that something was wrong.

"Actually, we seem to have misplaced something. If we send you some information could you discreetly ask the other Ambassadors to help locate it?"

Esther covered her face with her hands in disbelief at what Daniel had just told Gabriel.

"Of course. We can't have important items falling into the wrong hands, can we?" Gabriel replied letting Daniel know he knew what was missing.

"Thank you very much Gabriel, we will send the tracking information immediately."

"Good luck Daniel. We will do our best to help, we all know what will happen if you fail." Gabriel replied as the screen faded, ending the transmission.

On receiving the details of the tracking device IES organisations all around the world sprang into action. Ranger response teams on every continent were put on high alert. Using every satellite and receiver at their disposal every inch of land and water was covered as they waited for the tell-tale signal that would give away the book's location.

"I will contact Alice's family and give them the bad news. When I get my hands on whoever is responsible for this, they will wish they had never been born," said Esther as she walked out of the room.

Shortly after Esther left, Zhang Wei entered the room and walked over to Sonia. He whispered into Sonia's ear.

Sonia then announced to the remaining staff, "We have another problem. This is Zhang Wei and he has something to tell you."

Chapter 23

D aniel took Carla to the restaurant to get her a drink of coffee. It was deserted and they both sat down at a table, Carla sipped her coffee, her hands slightly trembling as she reconstructed in her mind all the things that had just happened. Daniel took her hand and asked if she was okay. Carla replied she was fine, but he could see the upset in her eyes.

"That man saved my life and that poor woman. Why?" Carla asked looking at Daniel.

"I'm sorry you had to go through this, maybe I should never have invited you." Daniel replied.

"But you did, and now my friend is God knows where with some crazy woman who tried to kill me."

"The night that we first met there had been a failed attempt to abduct me. We suspected that someone had learned of the existence of the book and needed me in order to obtain it," explained Daniel.

"You mean that book the professor was using?"

"Yes. For thousands of years the Shey Atar has visited this world, occasionally taking on a student. The students were usually women and they would be taught how to use all the natural things around them. For example, how to make medicines, grow food, use their emotions to communicate with other animals and even to an extent change the weather. Not on a massive scale, but enough to help them get by. They have watched humans for a long time and believe you have great potential. One student, Mary, wished to take her knowledge and travel South to help people who were suffering from a serious disease. The Shey Atar allowed her to take a book of symbols with her to assist, on the condition that she returned it. Mary had a thirst for knowledge and my Shey Atar shared many secrets with Mary, allowing her to take symbols that gave her insight into many secrets of the Universe, she could see other worlds and beings. Mary was the kindest of people and my Shey Atar loved her. Whilst she was on her travels she adopted three orphans, two girls and a boy. They eventually settled in an area that is now known as Canary Wharf in London. They lived amongst the locals and were highly respected for the knowledge that Mary brought with her. She helped many people, and some would come from miles around to see her. Unfortunately, dark times began to creep across the land and soon word of Mary's work reached the ears of the religious extremists called witch hunters. Mary was arrested and found guilty of witchcraft, so were her two adopted daughters. As punishment for being witches the girls were murdered in front of her, their throats were slit and shortly afterwards Mary was burned alive at the stake. The boy was spared on the condition that he testified that his mother and sisters were indeed witches. That was something for which he never forgave himself. Before she died Mary instructed her son to ensure that no one ever took possession of the book. She told him to bury it in a box, deep in the earth with her and the two girls as one day the true owners would come and retrieve it. The boy carried out his mother's last wish, digging deep graves and leaving no headstone so that no one would trace them. In the box with the book was his journal telling the terrible story of what had happened. In 1991 at a construction site in Canary Wharf the grave and the box were located and that is when IES took ownership of it. The covers of the book were of a black ebony type wood. Carved into the cover were waterfalls, a large obelisk protruding from the ground, mountains with large crystals and running the length on the left side was a spider. Its pages were bound by silk thread. Inside the pages were made of fine woven silk. On the pages were sketches of bizarre looking creatures, moons, stars and planets. Spread out on the pages between the sketches were the most beautiful intricate golden symbols. Mesmerising to look at, with an energy that touched your soul.

IES had been established for some time by then and I was already working in London. I spoke with my Shey Atar and persuaded her to allow us to keep the book and use it to help us in our work. The condition of retaining it was that it must only ever be used inside IES properties and never again to be allowed to fall into human hands. She wept when she saw the book, she remembered Mary, I think from that moment she began to doubt the potential of humans as they realised their fallibility." Daniel explained.

"So why do they want the book?"

"When certain symbols are placed in a certain order in the correct conditions, they can create materials that humans would kill for, such as oil, diamonds, plutonium and many more elements. I underestimated the greed of some people and how ruthless they can be. I failed to protect the book and if the thieves activate the symbols outside IES property the Shey Atar will know. The consequences will be swift and like you have never seen. The Shey Atar have power you cannot imagine. They can create entire galaxies or destroy them. I must contact them and try to explain that this is my fault."

"What will happen to you?" Carla asked, concern on her face.

"I don't know. If I can persuade them that this is an isolated group of individuals and ask for time to retrieve the book maybe they will not act. I will speak with Forcarbon of the Shey Atar," he replied.

"Is that the lady that I saw at the hospital?"

"Yes. She is one of many, they are all very different."

"I'm glad you are ok, I was worried. Esther will rescue Melanie; trust her she is good at what she does. Please tell her where I am going and I will try to return, if they allow me," he said.

"We can both tell her because I'm going with you," said Carla impulsively.

***

The Captain of the Royal Navy destroyer contacted IES control to tell them that as they were approaching the abandoned yacht it had exploded, what was left of it had sunk into the depths of the sea. It was obvious that Kaya had not left any evidence behind, she had made certain of that. The Captain also explained that the submarine which had surfaced was like nothing he had ever seen before. It was black with a smooth even skin. There was neither a propeller visible, nor any other form of an obvious propulsion device. A panel on the surface slid open, Kaya, her staff and the two captives entered, it then closed. Most curious of all was that the submarine was wedge shaped and did not show up on radar or sonar. The Captain promised that he would try and locate the vessel and contact them should he find it. Aidan thanked him for his assistance and promised to keep him updated.

Esther returned to the control room still speaking on her mobile phone. She told Aidan that she had taken calls from several heads of states and other IES centres. The explosions that were being broadcast by the media had made a lot of people concerned, including the Prime Minister. Esther did her best to reassure them that there was nothing to worry about and that it was just a protest group causing trouble, deciding not to reveal the truth to them just yet. Only the British Prime Minister knew what was really happening and of the casualties. Esther was hoping that Kevin's tracker would activate, and that they could retrieve the book without alerting the heads of any other states. She realised that this was a very risky strategy, however there was no point in causing people to panic, besides which there was nothing that they could do to help. IES had all the resources that she required, she just needed to know where and how to best deploy them. Aidan briefed Esther on the update from the Captain and informed her of the latest problem. The Chinese tree spider had escaped and Sonia and Zhang were attempting to locate it. According to Zhang, it will head for trees. "No kidding," said Esther, sarcastically. "And here we are practically across the road from Greenwich Park." Esther instructed Aidan to provide them with all the resources that they needed, and to monitor the emergency services channels, as sooner or later someone was going to report seeing a giant spider.

Esther glanced out of the window looking down at the police and army vehicles, the ambulances had long gone. She had been updated on the progress of the injured and they were improving well, nobody was too badly hurt. She knew that she had Carla to thank for that. Even the unconscious female was doing well. The Metropolitan Police Commissioner had assigned a senior officer and she was efficiently processing the scene. The two bodies had been removed to the mortuary and it was only a matter of hours before the repair teams could move in. Oliver and DI Burns were at the public entrance to the Centre, surrounded by exhibits that they had seized and were being packaged. She noticed how enthusiastic DI Burns was. She considered how well they worked together. Esther reflected on her time in the Secret Service, she thought of all the organisations that she had encountered over the years as she tried to fathom out who this group were. They were well organised and clearly well funded, the combined worldwide intelligence services must have something on them. Kevin's team were checking the images that they had captured from the CCTV and she was waiting for them to get back to her. She turned to see Daniel and Carla enter the room.

Chapter 24

The Professor and Melanie were led onto the submarine whilst Kaya followed behind. Both had been handcuffed and masking tape had been applied over their mouths during the journey from the Exhibition Centre. Melanie could see that the Professor was distressed and tried to reassure him by making eye contact as they made their way into the vessel. She listened to what their kidnappers were discussing, hoping to catch the odd word but was unable to understand as they spoke in Arabic, quickly realising that Kaya oversaw the others and directed them accordingly.

She then reflected on their own treatment. Apart from tying them up and taping their mouths their captors had treated them well. There was no pushing or shoving, and no threats had been made. As Melanie walked down a corridor which seemed to appear from nowhere on the side of the submarine she was amazed at the advanced technology and spacious inside area. She could tell by the Professor's expression of wonderment that he too was impressed by what he saw as he gazed around the interior of the vessel. They were both led to an informal reception area with seating and tables. A large black glass window on one side of the room gave a view of the underwater world through which they were currently travelling. Kaya removed the masking tape from their mouths and instructed them to sit on one of the large sofas. Still handcuffed they both sat down.

"The explosion I heard on the boat. Was that the IES centre?" Melanie asked staring intensely at Kaya.

"It was just a little something to keep them busy whilst we were leaving."

"If you have harmed any of my friends, I swear I will kill you."

"Aren't you a tough little pretty? I think you are no research assistant."

"Take these cuffs off and you'll see how tough I am you murdering savage," Melanie replied with a caustic smile.

"He was an unfortunate casualty," said Kaya, squeezing her hand tightly around Melanie's lower jaw.

Melanie dipped her head and bit into Kaya's hand. Kaya shouted out in pain and raised her hand to slap Melanie, who in turn instinctively closed her eyes in anticipation of the assault.

Almost immediately a deep male voice shouted "Kaya! Stop!"

Melanie opened her eyes to see a man had entered the room. Kaya lowered her hand.

"I will be seeing you soon my pretty little biter," said Kaya as she walked towards the man.

Melanie and the Professor both looked at him in surprise, and Melanie smiled to herself when she saw Kaya rubbing her hand where she had bitten her. The man was over six feet tall and stocky built. He had olive skin and black hair with grey streaks. He was aged in his late fifties and was immaculately dressed. His clothing was obviously expensive and made to measure, he wore a thick gold bracelet and a diamond ring on the small finger of his left hand.

Kaya looked at Melanie with a smile on her face. "We do not need her anymore, why not get rid of her now?"

"Do not harm her," replied the Professor.

"No one will be harmed. Kaya leave us," said the man.

Kaya turned back to look at Melanie.

161

"I think I may know someone who would love you to be part of their life. When I find them I will introduce you personally."

"Now Kaya!"

Kaya turned and left the room.

"What was that supposed to mean?" asked a puzzled looking Melanie.

"Pay no attention to her. I must apologise for forcing you to come here Professor, but I suspect that you would not have willingly visited me with the book. Melanie I am sorry you had to be involved however hostages are sometimes a necessity. Please make yourselves comfortable. You both have individual private quarters and are free to roam the Dragonfly as you wish. The crew have been told to answer any questions that you may ask; I have nothing to hide from you. I suspect Professor that you will find the Dragonfly most interesting. In your quarters there is an intercom, just ask for whatever you need. Please try to enjoy the journey, there is so much to see. During the next five days I will explain all and I hope Professor you will see our goals are very similar to those of IES."

He summoned one of his crew and told him to remove the handcuffs and show his guests to their quarters.

"Who are you? What is your name?" asked the Professor.

"I am known as The Bulgarian. Please do not try anything stupid I would not want any harm to come to either of you."

Their quarters were luxurious, and located next door to one another, both had dark glass panels from which they could watch the passing ocean and all its inhabitants. Melanie knocked on the door of the Professor's quarters, he opened it and invited her in.

"We never really had the opportunity to introduce ourselves. I was invited to the Centre with my friends

162

by Daniel. I am a Police Officer, but I suspect these people know that by now."

"I am pleased to meet you Melanie. I must admit you did not strike me as a lab technician when we first met."

"I'm sorry I called your experiment a piece of rock. Listen, there is obviously no way off this submarine, so we have no choice but to go along with what they want for now. I know that even as we speak now, IES will be working on a plan to secure our release."

"I'm not really that concerned to be honest, after all if they wanted to harm us, they could have done that already."

"You are right about that and I can't complain about the accommodation. This place is amazing."

"I agree, and I intend to learn as much as possible about this vessel whilst we are here."

"And I will learn as much as I can about our kidnappers."

"Melanie. Please stay away from that woman. I don't think she likes you very much."

"I will do my best but somehow I think that us meeting and clashing is inevitable."

Chapter 25

Greenwich Park is a beautiful place attracting thousands of visitors every year. In its centre is the world-famous Greenwich Observatory. Backing onto the West side of the park is a row of large Victorian detached houses in a tree lined street. A group of children were playing in a side alley between the houses when they noticed a dark shape moving behind the rubbish bins. As they drew nearer, they saw that it was a huge black spider. One of the children screamed and ran off whilst those remaining picked up stones from the ground and began to throw them at it as it crawled out from behind the bins. A more adventurous one took out his mobile phone and began to record the scene. The spider then ran up the wall of the nearest house and it disappeared inside through an open window.

***

Henry Jacobs was putting away the last of the dishes from the evening meal that he and his daughter had just eaten. Jessica, or Jess as she preferred to be called, was eight years old. A bright pretty girl, she adored painting. She was sitting at the dining table with her paint pot creating her latest masterpiece when her father Henry called to her.

"Jess finish up now it's time for bed."

"No just a little longer please."

"Jess, your mum will be back soon, and you need to be in bed. We have an early start tomorrow."

"Okay Daddy. Can you read me some more of Fearless Ferris Fumper please?"

"Of course honey. Now brush your teeth and get into bed and I will come up and read to you."

Jessica put away her paint set and climbed the staircase to the bathroom. She opened the door and pulled the cord to turn on the light. As she walked toward the basin something in the bath caught her eye. After thinking about what she saw for a few seconds, she considered what Fearless Ferris Fumper would do in this situation, but eventually decided to go and tell her father. Jessica walked back down the stairs into the kitchen where Henry was just finishing tidying up.

"Jess I told you to go to bed."

"But daddy, there's a spider in the bath."

"Don't be silly Jess. That spider is more scared of you than you are of it. Let's catch it and put it outside in the garden."

Henry opened a cupboard door and took out a glass.

"We can catch it in this and release it outside. Okay."

"Daddy you will need a bigger glass than that."

A few minutes later Henry ran from the house carrying Jess in his arms. Slamming the door shut behind him he ran to the house next door where his friend Marcus lived. He banged on the door frantically until Marcus opened it.

"Henry! What the hell's wrong?"

"There's a spider in my bath!"

"For God's sake Henry man up."

"No, you don't understand. It's big, really, really, big. Please take Jess I need to call the Police. Close all your windows Marcus."

Marcus invited them both inside and closed the door. He was not really sure what Henry was talking about; however, he could see the fear in his eyes. Marcus's son James on hearing the commotion came into the hallway. Marcus told James to close all the windows as Henry had asked. James looked at Marcus.

"Because of the spider?" asked James.

"You know about it?" said Marcus, inquisitively.

James took out his phone and showed them the video recording of the spider by the rubbish bins. He had already posted it on social media and had many hits.

"Oh my God. That thing is huge."

Henry was by now at his wit's end and called the Police.

"Emergency services, what is the emergency"

"There's a big spider in my bathroom."

"Is this some kind of a joke? It is a serious offence to waste police time."

"No! No! it's no joke this spider must be at least three feet long. I've never seen anything like it."

The operator took Henry's details and told him that an officer would come round but also warned that if this was a joke he would be in serious trouble.

At that moment Esther was pondering her next steps when one of Aidan's controllers called to her.

"Esther, we have our first spider call. A male states a three-foot spider is in his bath. The address is in Greenwich Town Centre."

"Good. Get Sonia and that scientist Zhang over there immediately. Hopefully they can contain it before the Police get there and shoot it or whatever it is that they do to large spiders. Send a small group of Rangers to assist them."

"Will do."

Sonia and Zhang arrived at the address to see Henry and Marcus standing outside in the next-door garden. Sonia looked at Zhang and asked exactly how are we going to catch this spider, even if we do see it? Zhang explained that he had already been in touch with the Chinese field crew and they were despatching a specialised container, but in the meantime, they would have to

166

improvise. Zhang walked back to his vehicle and opened the hatchback door. Sonia was somewhat taken aback as he walked back towards her carrying two large fishing nets.

Henry approached them and asked if they were the Police. Sonia showed him her warrant card and explained they were specialists and were here to capture the spider alive. Henry appeared quite surprised at how they took it all in their stride. The fact that there was a three-foot spider, something he had never heard of, in his bath, didn't seem to faze them. He handed them the door keys and explained where the bathroom was as they entered the house. They made their way to the bathroom and opened the closed door. The bath was empty, and the window was still open. The spider had escaped again. Sonia called control and gave them the news. She said they would stay in the area in case another call came in. They didn't have long to wait. Control also informed her that four IES Rangers were being despatched and they arranged to meet them.

***

Mrs Dolores Brown and her husband Derek were late returning home after spending the day with their daughter and her children in Woolwich. They often visited and spoiled the grandchildren; on this occasion they had been to a riverside restaurant for brunch and had enjoyed a lovely day in the autumn sunshine. Dolores had decided to make a roast chicken dinner, she put the bird in the oven and started preparing the vegetables and setting the table. Derek was in the garden shed pottering around. Two hours later Dolores took the cooked chicken from the oven and placed it on a plate on the dining table to rest and went to call him. He told her that he was on his way and Dolores returned to the dining room. She was just in time to see a large spider with the chicken in its mouth exiting the house through the open dining room window. The scream from the house caused Derek to rush indoors.

"A giant spider just stole my chicken!" Dolores shouted pointing at the window.

Derek peered cautiously out of the window just in time to witness the spider crawling along the wall with the chicken in its mouth.

"Well that's something you don't see every day."

He hurriedly called the Police to report what had just occurred. In turn, IES control advised Sonia of the latest call about a chicken eating spider, she, Zhang and the four Rangers made their way to the address, which was only a few doors away.

Derek pointed out the location where he had last seen the spider, and the direction in which it was heading. It appeared that it was making its way towards the trees that lined the park boundary. As the group headed towards the line of chestnut trees carrying their fishing nets, they were receiving strange looks from curious bystanders.

"It could be anywhere," said Sonia.

"We need to tempt it out with some food."

"It's just eaten a chicken."

"That doesn't matter, when they are young, they are voracious because they grow so quickly. It will be hungry again soon."

"How did you come to find these creatures? I've never heard of them."

"Legend has it that a group of Chinese Shamans living in the wilderness had become victims of attacks by groups of soldiers. Many were killed, but several managed to flee. Knowing the soldiers were not far behind they called for help from their priestess. As the soldiers approached an Angel appeared with an army of giant spiders. The soldiers turned and fled in terror and the Angel relocated the Shamans to an area deep into the wilderness where they were safe. She left the spiders to protect them. Whilst China was still in the IES program stories emerged of hunters killing gigantic spiders. I went with a field crew and we found them. I knew that China was about to abandon IES, so we began moving the spiders to safety in Edens all over the world."

"Fascinating. So, what does it want for dessert?"

"We need some fresh meat."

Sonia contacted IES control and asked them to arrange for some fresh meat to be despatched to the park as bait for the spider. She also suggested that they ought to get this area of the park evacuated by the Police. Aidan said that he would arrange for the park keepers to tell people that tree surgeons would be operating in the area and that it would need to be cleared and cordoned off but that may take a while to arrange. The two of them sat on a park bench with their fishing nets and waited. The four IES Rangers waited at a discreet distance, very shortly afterwards the four were joined by an additional Ranger with a piece of fresh meat.

After what seemed like an eternity one of the park keepers reported seeing something moving in the shadows at the foot of a tree. The duo jumped up and made their way to the location. They updated Aidan, who in turn updated Esther.

"Sonia and Zhang think they have spotted the spider. They are literally sealing the area off now. We have sent an additional Ranger with some fresh meat to assist".

"Meat?"

"They are going to try and tempt it out. It will smell the meat. They think it is in a tree somewhere.

"Okay. Let's get this thing caught. Sonia must be as tired as the rest of us."

In the meantime, the park keepers had cordoned off the area in the park where Sonia believed the spider had taken refuge. They had placed signs stating, 'Tree Surgery work in progress please keep clear', and it was obviously working as people were remaining outside the cordons.

***

At the edge of the cordon Mrs Joyce Goodwin was taking Pretty Poo, her toy poodle for their usual evening walk. She stopped and sat on a bench to chat to Mrs Alice Jones, a friend who was walking her own dog. Charlie Pooh was barking and pulling at her lead. "Calm down dear," shouted Mrs Goodwin, as she released some more slack on the extension. Charlie Pooh ran over to the base of a large tree, staring up into the branches and barking as the now perfectly camouflaged spider slowly descended the trunk. Mrs Goodwin again called to Charlie Pooh to calm down and continued chatting with Mrs Jones. All of a sudden, the lead pulled at her hand and as she turned round, she could see that the lead was now going straight up into the tree branches and Charlie Pooh had stopped barking. She ran over to the tree to establish how on earth her pet had managed to climb up it. In the dusky light she could make out the silhouette of Charlie Pooh dangling in mid-air from her lead, as if snagged on a branch. As she focused, she saw that the lead was in fact in the mouth of something big. Something unbelievable. Screaming for help she pulled at the lead with all her strength. Charlie Pooh fell from the branches and immediately ran over to Mrs Goodwin and jumped into her arms. Mrs Goodwin in turn, ran through the park towards Mrs Jones screaming, "Monster! Monster!"

Sonia, Zhang and the Rangers had heard the earlier commotion and were already on their way in the direction of the kerfuffle.

"Well that's our tree." said Sonia.

170

They ordered the park keepers to clear the area surrounding the tree and laid the meat on the floor about six feet from its trunk. With their fishing nets ready they watched and waited. One of the park staff approached Sonia carrying a large box that he had brought from their vehicle. He explained that Aidan had sent it as he thought it may be of use. Sonia opened the box and inside was a large net. Perfect, she thought, much better than these fishing nets. She asked the Rangers to unpack it and spread it out amongst them in order that they could throw the net over the spider as it ate. Zhang had taken a call from his team who confirmed that a container was en route and that that they would transport the spider once it had been captured. He stressed to Sonia that no harm must come to the spider. Everyone was now ready, silent and waiting. After a few moments Sonia spotted some movement in the leaves of the tree. Slowly the spider climbed down the tree and crawled across the grass, although it was still taking on the appearance of tree branches the movement gave it away. After a slight pause it began to move into the open towards the meat. Sonia saw her chance and ran towards the Spider with her net followed by Zhang. They both brought their nets down on the spider, Sonia catching most of its body and Zhang's net landing over the top of Sonia's. Startled by their sudden movement the spider began to run but it was strong and pulled them both to the floor. They both held on with all of their might, as they were dragged along the floor through the grass and mud. Zhang's net suddenly worked its way free, leaving just Sonia being dragged by the spider. Sonia's weight had slowed the spider down sufficiently for the IES Rangers to catch up and throw the larger net over it. They pinned the net down and although the spider struggled it was caught, so unfortunately was Sonia. She crawled out from under the net, covered from head to toe in mud and grass, giving Zhang a withering look as she did so.

"Can I go home now? I need a bath."

Chapter 26

In the control room the mood was sombre, hours passed with no news. Kevin was interrogating and cross-referencing intelligence databases as he attempted to establish the identity of any of the group involved in the attack. Aidan and his team were busy monitoring, waiting for any trace of the tell-tale signal, either from the submarine, or attempted use of the book. Esther was racking her brain trying to think of anything else that she could do when Kevin hurriedly entered the room.

"I've found something. The female popped up on an MI6 database, her name is Kaya Kouri."

"Well done Kevin. So, who is she? Where do we find her?"

"That's just it. When I tried to open the file associated with her it stated 'classified'. We are locked out."

"What do you mean locked out. We have access to any files on any system."

"I know but this one is locked out."

"MI6. I might have guessed. That spineless weasel. Leave this with me Kevin, I will acquire access. Just be ready to go through the files and locate this Kaya Kouri."

"We will be ready."

As Esther walked down the corridor towards the exit, she saw DI Burns helping Oliver, the botanical scientist walk towards the restaurant area. He had a tissue to his nose and his head was held back.

"Is everything okay?" asked Esther looking concerned.

"Yes, fine. He just tripped over one of the plant containers and hit his nose. He'll be fine."

Esther told them to take some rest and that she would get some more staff to help them moving the displays on her return.

She then left the office heading to her car. She was on her way to her old playground at MI6 to have a meeting with someone that she hadn't seen for years and had always hoped that she would never see again.

In the meantime, DI Burns helped Oliver to a seat, Oliver then called his wife to explain that he would be late home. Taking advantage of a few moments down time DI Burns called his own wife. He had already spoken to her earlier to re-assure her that he was fine, as the incident at the Centre had made the news. It was difficult for him to not be able to tell her what was really going on, but then he knew she would worry so much and for Melanie's safety he could not allow the truth to get out yet.

***

Esther pulled into the car park at MI6, a building that she had been to so many times over the previous few years. She parked her car and entered the building showing her pass when required, many of the staff recognised her from her previous role. She said the occasional 'hello' whilst making her way to C's office, one that she had once occupied. As she approached the secretary's desk, she saw a face that she recognised. Kendrik Tinkerstone was a slightly effeminate older gay man. Highly intelligent and incredibly efficient, he had worked for Esther for several years when she held the position of C.

Kendrick looked up at Esther as she approached.

"Esther! Darling it's been ages."

"Hello Kenny. How are you?"

"Oh, I'm fine. Nobody calls me Kenny anymore, not since you left. It's all Mr this and Mrs that now. Listen he knows that you're here, he instructed me to put an alarm on your pass. He said that he does not want to see anyone. Well fancy that?"

174

Kendrick glanced at his watch. "It's my coffee break, so I will just pop out for a moment." said Kendrick smiling as he walked towards the door.

"It's good to see you again Kenny."

"It's good to see you too Esther."

Esther opened the door to the main office and walked in.

"Esther. What brings you here?"

Esther walked over to the desk and sat down in the leather winged chair opposite C.

"Please will you unlock the files to which you have restricted IES access."

"I have no idea what you are talking about?"

"You are aware that IES is authorised access to any files on any system. Please stop the games and unlock the files."

"Esther. MI6 are here to assist IES in any way that we possibly can, you know that you only need to put in a request. I imagine that this is down to an administrative error. If you provide me with the file name, I will get IT onto it immediately. They are a bit short staffed at the moment, so it may take a little time. I will instruct them to make it their number one priority."

"Listen C, I don't have time for this crap, I have had members of staff kidnapped. If you want your lazy arse to remain in that nice chair start arranging it now please."

"Are you threatening me Esther?"

Esther did not reply. She simply reached over and took a page from a notebook on the desk. She picked up a pen, wrote one word on the paper and slid it across to C. He stared at what she had written, his face emotionless. C then picked up his telephone.

"Give IES access to the locked files."

"Thank you." said Esther as she got up to leave.

"It was a long time ago, and I wasn't responsible for that."

"Oh, I believe you C. The question is. Would they?"

Esther left the office and returned to her car. She called Kevin and told him to try and access the files again as access had been arranged and that she wanted a full briefing of the contents on her return. She then noticed that she had a text message on her phone. It was from an anonymous sender and it read.

'The Professor and Melanie are both safe and are being well cared for. They will be returned unharmed in six days. Do not attempt to locate them.' Esther forwarded the message to Daniel's mobile.

Chapter 27

D aniel and Carla left the Centre in Daniel's car heading back to his office. Carla took the opportunity to call Betty and reassure her that she was okay, Carla knew that news of the explosion had been on the television. Betty was pleased to hear from Carla and told her not to worry if she was not home when she got back as she was going to a yoga class then may attend a social evening at the local pensioners club. Carla could not help wondering what on earth the Shey Atar had given to her that evening at the hospital.

As they made their way Carla saw something black in her peripheral vision, it was moving quickly across the sky. As she turned to follow the shape, she saw a large crow land on a window ledge. She noticed that there were several more of the birds, they were gathering on lamp posts, rooftops and even on the pavement. How odd she thought.

"Harbingers of doom."

"Sorry Carla, what was that?"

Carla gestured towards the crows.

"Crows. Harbingers of doom. That's what my gran used to tell Stephen and me when we were kids."

Daniel glanced at the crows and then turned back to the road and continued with their journey.

"I know what happened to Stephen. I'm very sorry."

"It was a long time ago but thank you."

"You miss him a lot."

"Every day. So, do you carry out background checks on everyone you meet?"

"Only the important ones." Daniel turned and smiled.

Carla looked at Daniel as he was driving. There was something about him. Yes, he was attractive, but he was genuine, he really cared about people, yet despite his background he maintained an air of innocence. This is crazy, am I developing feelings for him she wondered to herself. They arrived at the IES building Daniel parked the car and they entered the reception. As they made their way to Daniel's office Carla could see that something was bothering him.

"What's wrong?"

"I don't want you to come with me. It could be dangerous."

"Why? I've seen her before."

"It's not just Forcarbon."

"Forcarbon? Is that her name?"

"In your language yes. Their name is what they are, what they represent, what they control. And there are many. I would not want anything to happen to you."

"I'm not letting you go alone. I'm coming with you."

"I knew that you would say that."

Daniel picked up his office phone and asked for arrangements to be made for two people to travel to Eden 7.

"Eden 7?"

"It's where I need to contact Forcarbon. It is an amazing place you will love it."

"I know you said they came to be, but came to be from where?"

"When we get to Eden 7, I will tell you the stories of the origins of my people. I will tell you how we all came to be and why the Shey Atar are here. I hope you like camping out in the wild, we may be gone for a few days."

"A few days. Yes, that will be nice, but I haven't brought any suitable clothing or anything with me."

"It will all be provided."

Carla looked at Daniel with a smile and a feeling of excitement at the idea of camping out in the wilderness with him. She sent Betty a text message to let her know that she would be staying with friends for a few days and not to worry.

"You know who would have loved to be doing this? Melanie. I hope she's okay."

"Esther will get her back. Believe me if anyone can, she can."

A call came through to Daniel's phone. It was to confirm that the helicopter was ready and waiting for them. They boarded, put on their headphones and they were off, heading North out of London.

It was a cold day with grey skies and a light drizzle as the helicopter touched down in a field area. They got into a waiting jeep which was being driven by a Ranger.

"Hello Daniel. Hope you had a pleasant trip."

"Hello Scott. It got a little bumpy at times. May I introduce Carla, she will be accompanying me into Eden 7."

"Pleasure to meet you Carla."

Carla smiled at Scott. She noticed a large wooden hut ahead of them just inside the fence area, which seemed extend for miles. As they drew closer, she could see the electrified fence signs running all along it and the danger sign saying *Army! Live ammunition in use.* The jeep pulled up outside two large gates which were opened by another Ranger. Scott drove inside and parked the jeep outside the hut.

"We have been expecting you. Your rucksacks have been prepared; they are inside. Would you like a coffee or anything?"

"No thanks Scott we need to get on our way."

"OK. I will just go and get your things."

Scott walked into the hut as the other Ranger was closing the gates. Carla looked out at the barren landscape. There was nothing but grassland as far as the eye could see. Why would anyone want to put an electric fence around empty land? she wondered.

"So, is this it? Is this Eden 7?"

"Yes. This is it."

"Oh. I don't really know what I was expecting, but this probably wasn't it. So, are we going to be camping in the middle of a field?"

"We have a short hike first, about five minutes and then we will be there."

"Be where? It's just an endless field. And is that fence really electrified?"

"Just a mild shock, that's all."

"Well this should be fun."

Scott then appeared with two large rucksacks and two pairs of boots. They both put on their boots. Perfect fit, he's even researched my shoe size Carla thought to herself.

"Will you be ok with that? It is a little heavy." Scott asked Carla.

"I will be just fine, thank you."

They both put on their rucksacks and said goodbye to Scott as they made their way into the huge field. After about five minutes Daniel came to a halt by a large boulder, half buried in the ground.

"Is this it? I mean I can still see the hut. Why don't we just stay in there?"

Daniel smiled at Carla and raised his right hand in front of him as if pushing a mid-air invisible object. She then saw a shape shimmer around his hand as if he had touched something. Suddenly an opening began to appear out of nowhere. It comprised two large doors, each at least twelve feet wide slowly opening. And where previously she could only see fields and sky, she could now see what was hidden behind this camouflaged wall. The wider the doors opened the more she saw, and it was wonderful.

"Oh my God!" she exclaimed.

They walked through the open doors which then slowly closed behind them, concealing their location to the outside world. They found themselves in a small clearing, there was a wooden building to their left it appeared empty and a metal wire fence and gate that separated them from the flora and fauna beyond. Daniel opened the gate and they walked into the forest area. Carla looked around at the beautiful selection of the most unusual plant life. Tall trees with large star shaped leaves bearing long orange coloured fruits, the floor was a carpet of colourful orchid type flowers with brightly coloured insects flying around them. A movement in a tree to her left caught Carla's eye and she noticed a small monkey disappear into the canopy.

"Daniel this place is beautiful. It's like a paradise."

"That's why we call them Edens. We bring the endangered species here to protect them until the world is safe for them to return. There are even some species in the Edens that humans believe to be extinct."

"Edens? There's more than just the one?"

"All over the world, hidden away."

"How have you managed this? I had no idea it was here from the outside."

"It is a technique that we use in my world. Do you recall the Chinese spider that you saw in the Centre? We collect its shed skin and grind it to a powder. When added to a liquid it can be poured into moulds. When dried it is incredibly strong but exceptionally light however it retains the ability to camouflage and blend in with its surroundings. The walls around this Eden are made of this substance."

Daniel led the way following a path through the forest. The noises, smells and sights filled her senses. After about fifteen minutes they came to the far edge of the forest and a large lake. Daniel pointed to their right where there was a tall rock ridge and told her that they were going to climb it and make their camp there. They navigated the narrow ledges which led to a flat clear area that ran into a cave. From the ledge Carla could see out across the whole of the Eden. "Wow, that view is spectacular," she said.

They entered the cave which was bare apart from a large stone alter. It was covered with the most intricate carvings. A small stone at the right edge of the table had four symbols carved into it. Daniel slid the stone to the left of the alter. The symbols glowed for a second.

"That's it. Now we must wait."

They unpacked their kit and set up the tents and sleeping bags. They had also been provided with a supply of food and drink. Daniel filled the small kettle with water and placed it onto the gas burner.

"Tea?"

"Yes please. So how long before Forcarbon shows up?"

"A day. Maybe longer. It depends what she is doing and how busy she is."

Daniel passed a cup of tea and a dried food packet of muesli bars and fruit to Carla. They sat drinking their tea and looking over the Eden as the sun began to set.

"It really is beautiful isn't it?"

Carla looked at Daniel and thought how content he seemed.

"Yes Daniel. It really is beautiful."

"Tomorrow if you wish we can walk to the other side of the lake. They have trees and bushes that bear the most delicious fruit."

"I would like that. It would be nice. You know if someone told me a week ago that I would be sitting here in a paradise with a total stranger trying to save the world I would have thought them mad. But here I am, it's like a dream, it is all just so surreal. But then I think of that poor man, Melanie, all those people in the Centre hurt and injured and realise it's not a dream it is a real-life nightmare isn't it?"

"I'm so sorry I dragged you into this Carla."

Daniel took Carla's hand and looked into her eyes. Carla knew he genuinely felt guilty about the whole situation.

"It's not your fault. Tell me about your home?"

Daniel sat back and thought for a moment, a smile crossed his face.

"My home world is a wonderful place. Two suns, three moons and the stars visible day and night. Endless forests of lush green trees with bounties of fresh tasty fruit, vast oceans and crystal-clear lakes. Creatures there that you would find bizarre, some of which are extremely dangerous. Oceans full of life and flying beasts as big as a house. My world is very ancient, the birthplace of all Shey Atar and symbols. It was the will of Atar that it should be."

Carla could see a distant sad look in Daniels eyes.

"Do you miss home?"

Daniel just smiled and took Carla's teacup which he topped up.

They made small talk and drank more tea before both retiring to their tents for the night. Carla was excited about the idea of exploring more of Eden 7, but could not help feeling guilty about being there whilst Melanie was who knew where? The text message that Daniel had earlier received from Esther made her feel more reassured. Their captors had clearly taken the time to let Esther know that the hostages were fine and being well treated, she hoped that it was true. Maybe it was down to the fresh country air, but Carla fell asleep within minutes of getting into her warm sleeping bag.

Chapter 28

Esther returned to the Exhibition Centre and made her way to the control room where Aidan and Kevin were waiting. It had been a long stressful day and she could see that everyone was tired.

"Esther. I have accessed the MI6 file and read the last document that was added. I can now see why they locked it. It wasn't just us that were locked out, it was everyone. Look at this."

Kevin passed her a document which she read intently.

"I can now see why he locked us out. He's not as stupid as I thought."

Esther asked Kevin to call his IT security department and put them on loudspeaker.

"Hello this is Esther. The file that we have just accessed is to be locked down immediately. No one, including me is to be given access to it. It will only be opened again when myself, Kevin and Aidan are present together and all agree. Please will you carry out an immediate level one security background check on myself, Kevin Hart and Aidan Preston.

Kevin and Aidan both looked at Esther in disbelief, they could not understand why she was checking on them.

"Don't you trust us?" asked Aidan with a puzzled expression.

"Trust does not come into it. As you just heard, you are also to carry out the same check on myself. The existence of the checks and the results are not to be disclosed to anyone. The three of us will meet here at ten o'clock tomorrow morning when you will provide them directly to us. Do you understand?"

"Yes Esther."

"Now you should all go home and get some rest. We will meet here tomorrow morning at ten. Aidan please nominate one of your staff to keep me updated on Sonia's progress. Good night gentlemen, I will see you in the morning."

At seven o'clock the following morning Esther was the first to arrive at the IES building where she headed directly to the conference room to await the arrival of the others. She sat down and started to read through an overview of yesterday's incidents. Kevin arrived at just before ten o'clock holding a cup of coffee and sat down at the table. They were both joined two minutes later by Aidan.

"Good morning gents. I am sorry to have to impose this on you, but we all have to be sure that we are completely security cleared before the contents of the file can be revealed."

Esther called IT security and asked them to deliver the results on speakerphone.

"Kevin level 1 background security check. Pass. Aidan level 1 background security check. Pass. Esther level 1 background security check. Pass."

Esther thanked the IT team and asked them to unlock the file and start to analyse its contents.

"I am sure we are all relieved to hear that we have all passed level 1 IES security. Now the reason that I had to be sure is that Kevin showed me a document from the file that MI6 had put together and hidden from us. It contained an extract of a conversation between a man known as The Bulgarian speaking to another man that he met in a restaurant last month. The meeting was recorded digitally, audio was impossible as the filters had too much background noise. They engaged a lip reader to transcribe the conversation. Here is the product.

The schematics have been (something) (something). The Englishman will deliver the software for CRESI and construction (something) (something) (something). Delivery of raw material to continue to Syria (something).

So, you see. Someone in IES has been providing information about Jim's work."

"Well we know that it is none of us. If the information is related to CRESI it must be one of Jim's team. With your permission Esther I will initiate covert security checks on all of his team."

"Of course, Aidan. Get straight on it."

"Esther now that the file is unlocked if it's okay with you, I will get back to my office and start working through it."

"Yes, please and ensure that you keep me updated on anything that you find. I will give Daniel a call and see how he is getting on. I just hope that he can convince them to take no action."

"Oh, and Esther we attempted to trace that text message that you received but as we all suspected it proved impossible."

"No surprise there but thanks for trying Kevin."

Kevin and Aidan left the room and Esther stared at the phone. There was a call that she needed to make, and she was not looking forward to it. Her instincts told her that this was about to get a lot worse. Esther picked up the phone and dialled the number.

"Good Morning. Mark Kelly's office, how may I help?"

"Good Morning Sarah, its Esther. Is he free?"

"Good Morning Esther. Just a moment I will transfer you."

"Esther good morning. How are you?"

"I am good thank you Minister. You asked me to call you."

"Give me a progress report on locating the book please."

"We have a file on an organisation called Enigma. It was being withheld from us by MI6. It is being interrogated as we speak, I am hoping it will provide us the location to which the submarine may be heading."

"Withheld from you? Do I need to speak to C about this?"

"No, I am very sure nothing like this will happen again."

"So, if you establish the location what's your plan? Do you need military support?"

"If it is where I suspect then we cannot afford to send in any military. It could escalate into war."

"So, what do you need?"

"Let me see what's in this file. I may need a covert special operations team, but I will let you know?"

"Okay. Keep me informed the PM is constantly on my back about this. Esther listen, we believe that word has got out about the book being stolen. The Americans are pushing us for a meeting. Be prepared for some difficult questions to be asked."

"I was afraid of that. I will keep you updated."

"Has Daniel made contact yet?"

"Not yet. We have CCTV monitoring so we will know when they arrive."

"Let's hope he can convince them to consider their options or everything we are doing will be purely academic."

"I'm confident that he will. We haven't broken any of the rules so we should be okay."

"I hope so, for all our sakes. Goodbye Esther."

"Goodbye Sir."

Esther spent the rest of the morning following her usual work routine. She decided to drive down to the IES centre for lunch and establish how well Sonia and Oliver were coping. She smiled to herself as she recalled the phone call that she had received from Sonia the previous evening. How funny it would have been to see Sonia covered in mud and grass, holding a fishing net. Sonia also told her that Zhang had successfully transferred the spider to Eden 3 and that all was well. She called Daniel who advised her that they were now just waiting for the Shey Atar to arrive. Esther sensed the mood in his voice, she knew he blamed himself for all of this and she was worried at what exactly he would offer the Shey Atar for them not to harm anyone. Esther reassured him that none of this was his doing and that once this mess was sorted out, she was looking forward to working with him again.

As she turned into the Centre car park, she saw Oliver and Sonia speaking to DI Burns and DS Carter by the entrance area. She walked over and greeted them and asked how things were going.

There were also still several people looking on, some of whom were just curious and some of whom were a small group of protestors. The protesters were a regular feature whenever they discovered any IES operations. They in fact knew very little of IES's work, but nonetheless felt the need to protest.

"The public areas are almost ready, and we could easily open tomorrow, however the private area still needs quite a bit of work." Sonia replied.

"All my botanical exhibits are now back in place. I agree with Sonia we are ready to go."

"And you DI Burns, what do you think?"

"Everything seems to be in hand. You have a small protest group over there but nothing out of the ordinary however I would recommend increased security, just in case."

Simon was drinking his coffee whilst discreetly observing the protest group. Something didn't feel right to him. He couldn't quite put his finger on it, a copper's instinct really. He then noticed one of the protesters peel off and slowly walk in their direction. Outwardly nothing appeared unusual, he was a smart professional looking man, but Simon's instincts told him better. He was about twelve feet from them when Simon saw the man pull a knife from his pocket and begin to run towards Esther.

"Look out! Knife!"

Simon ran straight at the man and rugby tackled him to the ground, he was just feet short of Esther. The others turned and looked on in disbelief as Simon wrestled the knife from the man's hand and pinned him face down on the ground with one arm twisted up his back. DI Burns ran over and helped Simon to restrain the man. Simon, by now, had one of his knees in the small of the man's back. He continued to struggle but was no match for Simon and the DI.

"Bastards. IES bastards. You ruined my company! You ruined my family! You ruined my life you bastards!"

"Shut it. You're nicked sunshine," shouted Simon as he snapped his handcuffs on the man and dragged him to his feet. Two Rangers then led him away whilst he was still shouting.

"Is everyone okay? Esther, I think he was after you."

Esther looked at Simon with an expression of complete calm.

"I am fine thanks Simon. This is not the first time that we have had attacks on IES staff. There are a lot of people out there who would like to see the disbanding of IES."

"Guvnor I will deal with this bloke at the nick. I will be on my mobile apart from during the interview. If you need anything just call, otherwise I will catch up with you later."

"Of course Simon, well done and great job, thanks."

Following the incident Sonia and Oliver appeared a little shaken, Esther reassured them and gave her authority for the exhibition to open the following day, wished them well and made her way to the control room. Aidan was in the process of checking that the security systems were all fully functional.

"Afternoon Esther, I saw what just happened out there. I have already increased security. Anyway, I was just about to call you."

"That is what DI Burns said just before the incident, good idea. I take it you have some news."

"Yes. Brandon Scott has gone missing. We can't find him anywhere. Even worse, during the kidnapping CRESI's entire database was downloaded."

"I guess we've found our Englishman. I can hardly believe it. Brandon has worked with Jim for years."

"We are attempting to track his digital footprint but so far nothing has shown up."

"Ok. Thanks Aidan, let's hope Kevin comes up with a location."

Chapter 29

By the time they arrived at Eden 7 Carla was exhausted from all the experiences of that fateful day and slept very well, even if it was in a tent. She put this down to a combination of clean country air, the stress of the day and the warmest most comfortable sleeping bag.

She and Daniel spent the following day exploring the West area of Eden 7. Carla was amazed at how vast it was and how unusual and beautiful it all looked. They picked fruit for the day's meals, swam in one of the lakes, climbed a very tall tree and watched the unusual wildlife go by. They even rescued a strange little mammal that had become entangled in a large ivy-like plant. Carla's mobile phone was full of photographs of Eden 7, there were even some selfies of her and Daniel messing about by the shore of the lake. Daniel caught a fish with a contraption that he made from twigs and that evening they had a fish dinner using a small wooden table and two folding chairs that were stored in the cave. They sat and watched the stars as they sipped a glass of brandy from the supplies that they had been provided with. Carla thought it strange that the temperature was always comfortable, not too hot but not too cold either. The events of the day eventually caught up with them, she estimated that they had walked about fifteen miles and after saying their good nights they once again retired to their respective tents. Carla considered how well Daniel coped in the outdoors and how much of a gentleman he was. 'I like him' she said to herself as she drifted off to sleep.

The following morning Carla woke to find that Daniel was already up. There was a pot of water boiling, she could smell the coffee that he had prepared and could see the fresh fruit breakfast that he had set out.

"Good morning. This looks lovely, I could get used to this."

"Good morning Carla, did you sleep well?"

"Yes thanks, that sleeping bag is so comfortable."

"Well eat up you're going to need your energy today."

"Why? What do you have planned?"

"I want to show you the South of Eden. You will need your rucksack and your hard hat."

"Climbing?"

"No, quite the opposite."

"Interesting."

Carla ate the healthy breakfast Daniel had prepared.

"That was delicious. Thank you. Daniel are you not worried that she hasn't responded yet?"

Daniel stopped what he was doing and looked at Carla. He could see her concern.

"I am not worried as I know that she will reply. She is rather busy, having a few universes to manage. Don't worry Carla, she will reply, I promise."

At the end of another full day of exploring they headed back to the ridge. Carla had enjoyed exploring the underground cave structures that looked so perfect, but so natural. Multi coloured crystals as tall as the Canary Wharf skyscrapers and small waterfalls, rock pools and streams. Daniel said that just like the ridge, they had created everything, but she was convinced he was only joking, there was no way they could have fashioned all that. As they approached the bottom of the ridge Daniel took hold of Carla's arm.

"I hope you have had a good time today?"

"Daniel it has been more than I could have ever wished for."

"Listen Carla. I know what happened with you before. The guy who hurt you and your grandma."

Carla stared at him intently, her smile fading.

"How dare you pry into my private life without my permission? Even after I tried to help you when most people would have backed away? What is my reward? Your organisation blackmail me and threaten me with losing my job. Well that is not how we get to know each other in my world."

Carla turned and began to walk up the ridge ledge. Almost immediately there was a loud bang and a bright light appeared from the within the cave and then faded away. They both stared at the cave entrance and Carla walked back into Daniel's arms as she saw what appeared.

"Oh no!" Said Daniel with a concerned look on his face.

"Let me guess? Forfire?"

They slowly made their way up the ridge ledge to where Forfire was waiting. Carla stared, her mind was in a mixture of disbelief and terror at what she saw. The heat is what hit her first, even down on the ledge you could feel it radiating. Forfire stood at least ten feet tall, her skin was grey but emitted a red glow. She sported a huge mop of wild black hair with sparks crackling, she wore flowing grey robes that moved around in the heat thermals. Her most striking features were her eyes of pure fire. Daniel knelt before her and Carla quickly followed. Forfire glanced at Carla then looked back at Daniel, it was as if Carla was of no importance.

"Why do you summon us Daniel?"

It was obvious that Daniel was afraid of her, he and his kind always had been. He summoned the courage to answer.

"I wish to speak with Forcarbon."

"Forcarbon is busy. You will speak with me."

Daniel had no choice but to speak to her. He knew that she was no friend of humans and would gladly have them removed if she had a reason. But he had to tell her, she could incinerate this Eden in a second if she wished. In reality, she could incinerate the entire planet.

"You dare not answer me?"

Carla saw the fire in her eyes grow brighter and the heat was becoming almost unbearable. Daniel looked at Carla and mouthed the word sorry. He turned back to Forfire but before he could speak a flash of light came from the cave and to Daniel's relief out walked Forcarbon. Carla immediately recognised her from Irene's description of the woman that she had seen at the hospital with Daniel.

She looked around as she assessed the situation then walked over to Forfire. Carla watched as they spoke for a few seconds then Forfire glanced at them both and walked back into the cave. There followed another flash of bright light which faded away to darkness, they both knew she was gone because the temperature began to drop immediately. Forcarbon looked at Daniel and Carla and smiled.

"Get up both of you. You do not need to kneel before us. You are creations of Atar, as are we all. Now Daniel why did you summon me?"

They both stood, Carla brushed the dust from her knees and noticed their small table and chairs were still smouldering, and the sweet smell of burning wood hung in the air. Daniel explained the situation concerning the book and took full responsibility, begging Forcarbon not to punish everyone else for his mistake. Forcarbon walked to the ridge edge and looked out across the Eden. She contemplated what Daniel had told her then called them both over.

"It is beautiful, and this world could be beautiful again, I really believe that. However, many of my sisters do not have my faith. They view humans as destructive, poisonous, almost a disease. Daniel listen, very soon humans will make an amazing discovery. They will find something that will allow them to travel beyond the stars, to other worlds and meet other beings. Some of my sisters believe they should be stopped before they damage other worlds as they have their own. But I tell them of the progress they have made since our Ambassadors were assigned and I believe that they will continue to improve. You must prove my sisters wrong, show them the good that you can bring. Return the book to me in three days and I will remove it from earth forever and keep it safe. Its potential is far too powerful to trust people to use it. Forfire is suspicious and will be watching, I can distract her but only for a few days. Now go, bring me the book. I cannot help you with this, my sisters will not allow it."

Daniel thanked Forcarbon and they both prepared to leave the Eden.

"Daniel. Make sure no harm is caused by the symbols in the book. If harm is caused and my sisters sense it then I will be unable to prevent them from following through with the threat."

They said goodbye to Forcarbon and left Eden 7 making their way back to IES London office. Daniel called Esther and briefed her on his meeting.

Chapter 30

Esther prepared to deliver her update to the representatives of the countries still committed to the IES treaty. Over the years for one reason or another some countries had abandoned the project, leaving parts of the globe with no IES foothold at all. Predictably, almost all the Middle and Far East had walked away from the treaty. One by one the video screens activated as the representatives appeared from around the globe. The UK's Prime Minister had already apologised to the other nations for keeping them in the dark about the stolen book. He explained that he was concerned an Ambassador of the Shey Atar may warn them before Daniel had had a chance to remedy the situation and promised that in future they would be fully updated on the progress. All the participating countries had now logged into the video conference meeting and Esther prepared to update them.

"Ladies and Gentlemen thank you for attending this meeting. I can tell you that the covert tracking device on the book was activated some hours ago and we now know the location of the submarine and its possible destination. On the map on your screen you can see from the last transmission the vessel was heading through The Straits of Gibraltar. According to the intelligence that we have gathered on Enigma we believe the destination is a port in Syria."

"Why did we not stop the submarine when we knew its location and before it got through The Straits?" asked the Spanish representative.

"The transmission only lasted for just short of five minutes before cutting off. It only transmits a signal when the book is opened, so it must have been opened briefly and then closed again. Also, we still have no way of tracking this submarine, it is invisible to all our detectors. MI6 have deployed an undercover agent who is currently working at a storage base at the port. It is also owned by Enigma and it appears as if they have moved into the area of toxic waste recycling. Diplomatic attempts with Syria to request Enigma hand back the book and hostages have failed, and it is only a question of time before they attempt to use it. The agent has delivered several waste containers including one into the port itself. We believe this port to be the book's final destination and will be our target. The agent reports that the only way in or out is through a large retractable door made of six-foot-thick concrete and moved by internal hydraulics."

"We cannot deploy military hardware into Syria, it is far too volatile, and the consequences would by catastrophic," stated the French representative.

"Agreed. We cannot use military force to get through that door. Missiles will leave evidence of external military involvement and the way things are now it would throw that region into war. We have a plan to get through the rock door when it is opened, for that we need covert specialist operations teams waiting. The interior is heavily guarded, and we also have two hostages to recover alive."

"I think I speak for everyone here when I say we will provide the best operational support teams in the world." added the American President.

"Thank you, Mr President. I will privately call you following this meeting to establish your Special Operations single point of contact. Aidan will be our single point of contact on this one. Ladies and Gentlemen as Daniel advised we have been given three days to recover this book. Thank you for your assistance and we will keep you all posted on the progress of Operation Firestrike."

Kevin returned to his office where he continued analysing the documents that they had received from MI6. Aidan immediately contacted the American Special Operations and they immediately start discussing a plan to get through the door. Esther requested that they held a short update meeting after lunch.

In the IES conference room Esther, Kevin and Aidan were joined by video link by the Prime Minister.

"So, gentlemen we know the target and we cannot risk waiting as it is almost certain that they will attempt to use the book. The problem that we have is how to get through that stone door without leaving evidence of military involvement."

"Considering the situation does it matter if we leave evidence." asked Kevin.

"It would lead to World War 3." Esther replied.

"What about The Reformers. I mean they built the ridge and cave structures in Eden 7 and the canyons at Eden 5. This would be easy for them." suggested Aidan.

"They are just kids Aidan."

"With all due respect Esther, you won't find a tougher bunch of kids than these. Besides all they need to do is take that door down. Special ops teams can do the rest."

Esther thought for a moment. Unsure if she should risk the lives of what some people would describe as children. Imagine the political fallout if things went wrong. No one would consider that the risk was proportionate to the many lives that depended on the success of the operation.

"Okay. Get your team ready Aidan. But they bring the door down and then they are out. I am very clear on this. No heroics. You understand?"

"Of course."

"In the meantime, speak to the Americans and formulate a plan for once we are in".

Chapter 31

The IES Reform Training Centre was located on the outskirts of Boughton in Kent. It was a fairly modern looking white metal and light blue panelled low rise building in lawned gardens with an enclosed courtyard out of public view. To the casual observer it was a nondescript office block. Aidan drove from London pondering throughout the journey whether in suggesting that The Reformers be deployed he had made the right choice. He entered the training room where five reformers waited, they stood to attention as he entered. How different they were from his first encounters with them, and how proud he was of every one of them. Jamal Khan was the senior reformer of the group and gave the order attention when Aidan arrived. Aidan remembered when he first met Jamal. The reform program was in its infancy and Aidan visited youth offenders' institutions across the country searching for potential program candidates. Aidan was at HMYOI Rochester speaking with the Governess and looking through the files of her current residents.

"Tell me about this one. He should have been released ages ago."

"Ah Jamal. He's a bit of a conundrum. A role model inmate for his term yet as he approaches his release date he gets into trouble and is given another sentence. It's as if he doesn't actually want to get out."

"Has anyone asked him why?"

"I have tried but he just locks up. No explanation."

"I would like to meet him."

"I will arrange it for you."

"Just me and him in a room. No cameras, no video, no guards."

"Aidan that is highly irregular, but what IES wants it usually gets."

Aidan was led to an interview room with just a desk and two chairs. The room was bland with pale blue emulsion walls, grey concrete floor, and a high white ceiling with fluorescent tube lighting. Jamal was sitting in one of the chairs as Aidan walked in. The guard locked the door behind him, and Jamal stood up.

Aidan smiled as he looked Jamal up and down. He was a smart presentable young man but had a sad almost tortured look in his eyes.

"So, Jamal, please sit down and tell me, what's your story?"

"I'm sorry sir I don't understand."

"You should have been out of here over a year ago. Yet every time you're due to be released you get into some kind of trouble. Why?"

Jamal just stared ahead and gave no answer. Aidan placed a picture of a young man on the table.

"Remember him?"

Jamal just continued to stare straight ahead.

"Look at it!"

Jamal glanced at the picture then looked away.

"Yes, you remember him don't you. How old would he be now? Eighteen, maybe have a girlfriend, a career, what might he be doing? The kid that you murdered."

Aidan pushed Jamal hard in the shoulder.

"Are you listening to me murderer?"

"Don't do that"

"Oh, tough guy. You can kill an unarmed innocent kid, how about take on someone bigger. Come on tough guy."

Aidan again pushed Jamal on the shoulder, this time so hard that he fell off his chair. Jamal jumped up and shouting in anger ran at Aidan. Aidan was ready for him punching him in the stomach and Jamal fell to the floor winded.

"So tough guy what is your story. Why are you still here?"

"They didn't punish me enough!" Jamal shouted, tears of frustration running down his face.

"Well there's something we both agree on. Get up and sit on the chair."

Jamal sat down on the chair, his stomach still aching from the punch.

"The thing is you didn't murder him did you. I have studied your case file. From what I read you were there but did not wield the knife or even touch the victim. You were charged under joint enterprise legislation. So, what's with all this pathetic self-pity?"

"I didn't try and stop it."

"Listen Jamal. You can rot in this place feeling sorry for yourself for all I care, or you can try and make amends. You can come and work for me and when I say work, I mean work. You will be exhausted every day, seven days a week. And on the rare occasion that you have a day off you will spend it working for a charity. But believe me when I say there are no second chances. You mess up and you will be out on your own and I won't care what happens to you. Stick with me and just maybe you will be able to look at yourself in the mirror again and have a little pride. The choice is yours. Think carefully about it. Here is my business card, if you are interested in my offer hand it to the Governess."

Aidan knocked on the door and the guard let him out. Days went by and Aidan had almost given up on Jamal until one morning he received a telephone call from the Governess.

"I have arranged an escort. Jamal is on his way to you. Good luck."

***

Aidan was not disappointed. Each reformer had their own harrowing story however Jamal worked hard and became one of the best reformers in the program and a good friend. Jamal was a natural, fully utilising the resources at his disposal including the newly designed suits, eventually he was appointed head trainer. One occasion, Aidan recalled, Jamal was instructing some new recruits, it was the first time that they had worn the suits. They had all completed the theory exercises and understood how to operate them but as Jamal said theory is one thing, it's getting into the suit and mastering it that is the real challenge. Jamal looked at the four trainees already in the black, leather body suits. Down the left arms were a series of gold symbols.

"The first thing we need to do is connect you to the suit. When you fasten your collar, you will feel a slight pressure on the back of your neck. That is your suit connecting to you. Stay focused and remain calm. When you are ready fasten your collars."

They all fastened their collars and Jamal saw in their faces that they could feel the suits connecting. All seemed to be going well until Jamal noticed that Katie Jones was becoming agitated.

"I don't like this. Get it off."

"Katie just relax it won't harm you."

Unfortunately, the pressure on the back of Katie's neck brought back the horrendous childhood memories of when her stepfather would grab her by the back of the neck and throw her against a wall. The overwhelming desire to run away swept over her.

"No, I don't like it. I don't like it! I have to get it off!"

Before Katie could unfasten the collar the suit had responded to her emotions. She flew straight up in the air, going higher and higher as her desire to run away increased."

204

"Oh no!"

Jamal flew straight up at an incredible speed eventually catching up with her he held her by the arms, they were both still ascending at great speed.

"Katie look at me. You have to stop panicking; we are going too high."

"Jamal I can't stop it. I can't stop it."

"Yes, you can. Katie trust me. You are with us now. We are your family and we will not let anyone ever hurt you again. I promise you. Katie you have to concentrate on your breathing, slow deep breaths."

"I can't do it."

"Katie we are going too high. There is no air up here we will die, you have to stop."

"I can't. You go. Leave me."

"I'm not leaving you Katie. I'm staying. If you die then so will I, but I won't leave you."

They began to slow down and finally came to a stop hovering thousands of feet in the air.

"Good Katie, well done. Shall we go back now? It's a bit chilly up here."

Katie smiled as she looked around and saw the curvature of the Earth.

"It's beautiful."

"Yes, it is."

They both slowly descended back to earth hand in hand.

***

Aidan scanned his six recruits one by one as they were sitting waiting for their briefing. Was this a good idea? Maybe Esther was right, they were just kids. He decided that he would explain the plan to them including their involvement and the risks involved, he would then allow each to make an individual

205

decision as to whether they wanted to take part in the operation. Their decision was unanimous, they all said yes. Aidan experienced a warm feeling of pride, considering what they used to be and where they came from, compared to what they are now. There was no time to waste. The training had to begin immediately.

Chapter 32

I t was the captives third day aboard Dragonfly, how surreal the entire situation was, thought Melanie. The crew were friendly, helpful and informative, not at all like the baddies that you see in films as she had initially imagined. The first day they spent most of their time together in Jim's quarters avoiding everyone and both feeling extremely nervous about their circumstances. On day two Jim suggested that they should venture out of their cabins and look around. To their surprise no one seemed to care at all as they just wandered around the submarine. The crew would say hello in passing, Melanie realised that was exactly what they were, just crew. Nobody monitored them or bothered questioning where they were going. The only exception being Kaya and her cronies, they mostly kept themselves apart from the rest of the crew, preferring to stay in their own quarters, which suited Melanie and Jim.

The submarine was huge, the rest of the quarters were towards the front of the vessel along each side of the corridor. There was a large gym, rest area and restaurant all in the lower section towards the middle. The top section had an amazing viewing area and scientific research centre. The navigation was at the rear and looked more like a science fiction spaceship. The captain sat in a huge leather chair in the centre of a circular control room with two similar but smaller chairs, one either side. The entire control room could rotate through 360 degrees. It had control panels in front of all three chairs which were touch screen operated. Jim was absolutely overwhelmed by the entire operation. The captain was an imposing Dutchman standing over six feet tall with white hair and a beard. He completely fitted the stereotype of an old sea captain. Originally from Domburg in Holland he had many years of seafaring experience. He had a deep booming voice and from his entire demeanour it was obvious that he was in charge as soon as you either saw or heard him.

"Jim, Melanie, welcome aboard I hope your accommodation is satisfactory."

"Yes, thank you." Jim replied.

"My name is Captain Max Visser, I know that you are not here by choice but whilst you are our guests, we will do our best to ensure that you are comfortable."

Captain Visser shook Jim's hand with a vice like grip which caused a little grimace. He then took Melanie's hand and gave it a gentle kiss. Jim and Melanie exchanged glances.

"Anything you want, please just ask."

"How about being set free?"

"Ha Ha Ha. Jim you are funny."

The Captain gave Jim a friendly slap on the back. Jim thought his shoulder might be dislocated.

"Melanie if any of these dogs give you any trouble you let me know. If they cause you any problems, I will have them flogged!"

"I think I can handle myself thank you."

"Ha Ha Ha. So I've heard." The Captain gave Jim another friendly slap on the back, walked over and sat in his chair.

"Melanie. Remind you of anybody?"

"The cartoon or the frozen food?" she replied smiling.

Captain Visser answered all of Jim's questions and there were many. The captain explained to Jim that the ship was powered by four magnetic field generators one at the front and back and the other two top and bottom in the middle of the submarine. There were magnetic field detectors all around the hull with a range of two thousand kilometres. The power came from two cylinders running the length of the submarine containing a mineral recently discovered while the company was drilling for oil. The only thing that the Captain could not elaborate on were the mineral details which he was under strict instructions not to divulge. Jim looked at the Captain, his facial expression showed that he had just realised something important.

"If this submarine manoeuvres by magnetic waves then......."

"Yes Jim? Go on," replied The Captain, smiling.

"Oh my God! This vessel can fly."

"Ha Ha Ha. Well done. Yes, it can and a whole lot more."

Jim pondered the latest revelation then looked at Melanie.

"Melanie do you realise what we are travelling in?"

"A flying submarine?"

"Not just that. If I'm right this vessel is also capable of space travel."

Jim looked back to the Captain who was smiling.

"Correct. In fact, as part of its development we have travelled to the dark side of the moon and back."

"So, the stories that I have read about sightings of a black triangular shaped object moving slowly across the sky were Dragonfly?"

"Yes, or one of her prototypes. We tried to keep her a secret, but obviously there were occasional sightings by ufologists. Fortunately for us, they are mostly written off as conspiracy followers and nutcases, and since she cannot be detected by radar or sonar there is never any evidence to back up the claim."

Jim could hardly contain his excitement at these revelations and appeared to have forgotten the fact that they had recently been kidnapped.

Jim spent the rest of that day talking with Captain Visser while Melanie decided to look at the gym. Melanie had been working out for about 30 minutes when Kaya walked in.

Kaya nodded in acknowledgement before selecting a fit ball at the other side of the room, and starting a sit up routine. After about fifteen minutes Kaya walked across to a set of gym mats that were already laid out, she walked over to a rack by the wall and picked up a stick.

"Do you Kendo?"

"Hai. Kekkō." *Yes. Very well*. Melanie replied in Japanese.

Kaya's face showed that she was impressed with Melanie's grasp of the Japanese language. She selected a second stick and threw it to Melanie. The fight was fierce with the sound of the clashing sticks ringing out around the gym. Some of the crew began to drift in, standing and watching, drawn by the women's shouts and the loud collisions of the sticks. They both took full advantage of the mat space forcing each other to move back and forth with each attack. The first strike went to Kaya, catching Melanie on her left shoulder, Kaya didn't hold back, and a searing pain shot down Melanie's arm, not that she displayed it. The second strike again went to Kaya, this time she struck Melanie's back. Melanie winced in pain but became more determined, remembering her father's advice that she must always remain calm and in control no matter what the situation. Kaya, by now confident that Melanie was no match for her, went in for her third strike. But this time Melanie was ready and determined to fight back. By this time a large number of the crew had gathered at the doorway and were watching with interest. Kaya lunged at Melanie, but Melanie spun round low and then rose up smashing the stick from Kaya's hand, then in another twist brought the stick swinging round stopping just millimetres from Kaya's throat. Third strike and bout to Melanie.

Kaya could hardly contain her anger and stared intently at Melanie. There was silence as their audience waited to see what was going to happened next, they were all aware of Kaya's violent reputation. Before things could degenerate and get out of hand The Bulgarian, who was by now in the audience, began to clap.

"Well done ladies a very impressive display. Now go and get ready, I want you to join me for dinner tonight. Melanie please also invite Jim."

The situation had been diffused, the pair nodded to one another in acknowledgement and made their separate ways out of the gym, back to their quarters.

At 8.00 pm that evening The Bulgarian, Jim, Melanie and Kaya sat at a large circular dining table which was perfectly laid out.

"I am sorry I have been unavailable since we left London, but I have had some issues to deal with. I hope your accommodation has been satisfactory."

"Considering the circumstances. Yes, it has been more than satisfactory. I just wish you would tell me what you want with me. I've seen the technology on this vessel, and it is way beyond anything that I can assist you with," replied Jim in an exasperated yet somehow excited tone.

"I think the crew are nice, and I had a brilliant workout today," said Melanie glancing at Kaya.

"Jim. We need your help with something quite different and when you see what we have planned I like to think you will agree with us. The end results are goals that both my people and IES are looking to achieve."

"Has it occurred to you that our friends and family may be worried about us? And what is your name, we can't just call you The Bulgarian."

Kaya stared at The Bulgarian with a cautious look as if he should not answer.

"You can call me Kal. Don't worry we have told IES that you are safe and well and that you will both be returned unharmed in two days."

"Assuming that I cooperate? Correct?"

"Jim when you see what we have to offer and the subsequent benefits to the world I am sure that you will help us. We arrive soon and all will be explained. Please understand that we are not the bad guys that you may think we are."

"So murdering and kidnapping people and placing explosives makes you the good guys?" said Melanie looking inquisitive.

"Melanie. We are a collection of people and organisations that own almost all the world's industries. We exist to maintain stability and economic strength, to threaten them are cardinal sins within our organisation. Yes, we make a lot of money, but we also keep millions of ordinary people in employment, we give them a future, normality, security. Unfortunately, there are people that try to destroy that. Terrorists, rogue governments, anarchists and that is where the likes of Kaya come in. They are necessary, they help us maintain order."

"Then why don't you share this amazing technology. You could wipe out fossil fuel pollution overnight."

"Jim, you are a brilliant scientist, but I am afraid that you are no economist. Just imagine if we did that. Overnight millions of people in the oil and associated industries would become unemployed. The knock-on effect would be poverty, despair, violence and then initially riots, probably followed by wars. No.

New technology needs to be introduced slowly to allow people and societies to adapt, to adjust. People basically hate change, especially if it makes them feel vulnerable."

The crew served them during the meal to a standard that many restaurants would be proud of and most of the evening the conversation was between Jim and Kal about Dragonfly. Following a glass of limoncello they all retired to their respective quarters. Kal suggested they both get some rest as they would be arriving at their destination soon. Neither Jim nor Melanie slept very well that night, anxiously wondering what lay ahead.

Chapter 33

The Reform Team had been thoroughly briefed and they were aware of the strategic aim, and their individual and team roles in the operation. They all sat together in the military aircraft which was now transporting them to Cyprus. It was dark in the hold area apart from the instrument lights that were flickering in the cockpit.

Aidan looked around at his team, the noise of the engines made it all so real now, they were on their way and he again wondered whether he was doing the right thing. They were sitting in silence, the atmosphere was sombre, with an atmosphere of nervousness. He looked around at Jamal, who had exceeded all his leadership expectations. Katie, considering her terrible abusive past, had settled in very well now that she had a true family. Aidan felt the anger still inside him when he looked at twin sisters Sanjeet and Anoor. Both were convicted of grievous bodily harm. At their trial neither would explain why they did what they did to their uncle, but both received a substantial prison sentence. Similarly, as neither had agreed to provide a victim statement, their uncle walked away with some injuries but no prosecution. In reality, he would have liked to have walked away, but after they had finished with him, he would never have sex or walk unaided again. Aidan recalled how after gaining their trust Sanjeet confided in him that one of the sisters had suffered years of abuse and agreed to comply and say nothing so long as the uncle never touched the other sister. Of course, the other sister eventually suspected something was wrong and the truth came out. After the tears and pain came the revenge, but she would never say which of them was abused. Then there was Mikey, a smart likeable kid. He spent most of his life being shifted between care homes and foster homes, never staying anywhere for more than a few months. Mikey was just a lost soul eventually getting involved in petty crime he was just drifting, and eventually found himself in a Young Offenders Institution, Aidan gave him a purpose and he did not disappoint.

Aidan caught Jamal's eye; he had also noticed the mood. Jamal looked at Sanjeet who was sitting next to her twin.

"Hey! Sanjeet. How you doing?"

"We are both fine, just want to get there and get this over and done with."

It was odd that whenever you spoke to one of the twins, they always replied for both of them, it was almost as if there were two physical people but only one mind. Jamal smiled and turned to Mikey who appeared deep in thought.

"Hey Mikey, you ok?"

"Razor."

"What?"

"Razor. My codename is Razor."

"Mikey what are you talking about?"

Mikey looked around at the others who were now all looking at him quizzically then turned back to Jamal.

"Well if we are going to be doing this whole save the world thing then I want a codename. And I want Razor because I am so sharp and besides it's cool to have a codename."

"Mikey don't be ridiculous."

"Hold on. If he gets a codename, then so should we. Me and my sister will be ..."

Sanjeet thought for a while and then said.

"Hailstorm and Thunder."

The twins looked at each other and smiled. The four reformers were now staring at Katie waiting for her response. Katie saw them and knowing what they were all thinking pondered for a moment.

"Okay. My codename will be Ghost, because they won't see me coming."

Jamal could only shake his head as Aidan laughed. Even though Jamal did not suggest a codename the team created one for him. He would be known as Alpha and even Jamal had to admit that codenames were an inspirational idea. Their spirits were lifted as they sang the reformer team song as they continued their flight to Cyprus, where they would be based on HMS Manchester which was waiting off the coast.

Chapter 34

M elanie was sound asleep when the sound of her alarm woke her. She looked at the clock which displayed 8.00 am then heard the announcement from the loudspeaker.

"All personnel. All personnel. Dragonfly docking in forty five minutes."

Melanie could hear a commotion outside her quarters, she got out of bed, showered and dressed. As she exited her room she could see Jim was already dressed and waiting outside his door.

"I guess we are almost there Jim?"

"Yes, it would appear so."

They made their way to the control area; both were feeling quite anxious as they had no clue as to what was going to happen next. Kaya stopped them halfway down the corridor and told them to go back and wait in their quarters and that they would be called when the vessel had docked. The forty five minute wait in Jim's quarters seemed to last forever when suddenly a knock came on the door. It was a crew member advising them that they could now leave the Dragonfly.

They followed the crew member who led them off the vessel and into a large docking bay inside an underwater cave. The submarine was surrounded by metal platform walkways, they were led along a walkway further into the cave and then up a staircase leading to a higher-level platform. As they looked over the handrail, they could see Dragonfly docked below. Jim was impressed at its sheer size and beautiful sleek design. A metal door slid open and they walked into a large room with desks and chairs. Several people were sitting at the desks working on computers and Kal was sitting at the far end of the room. He beckoned them over.

"Jim, Melanie. Please come, sit."

They took their seats and noticed that the windows of the room overlooked the opposite side of the docking bay where there was a large cargo holding area built inside the rock. Hundreds of roll-on, roll-off containers were stacked next to a crane on a rail track, which was obviously used to manoeuvre them.

"What is this place? Where are we?"

"Jim you are in our processing compound in Syria. We purchased this from the Syrian government. It was originally a military compound built into the rock to securely house treasures and gold during the last conflict. As you have seen it has an underwater port so that submarines could transport the items if required. Fortunately for Syria they were not"

"Syria!?"

"Downstairs is the process control area and that is what we need your help with. Once complete, you and Melanie can be on your way home."

"I wish you would explain exactly what you want with me."

"I will do better than that Jim, I will show you. Follow me."

They left through another door which led to a lift and descended into the cargo area, walking past the stacks of containers they turned a corner, Jim could not believe what he saw.

"Good God! I can't believe it."

Melanie saw what Jim was staring at and then turned back to him.

"Isn't that your machine from the Exhibition Centre?"

"Yes. Yes, it is. So, this is what this is all about? You just want to create more gold and oil. Don't you have enough?"

"Jim, you are still no economist. Now why would I want to destroy the price of oil or gold by flooding the market. No, we intend to use it for something quite different. For years people have tried and failed to create a clean energy source. We have discovered one but have been unable to introduce it. In the meantime, hazardous, toxic and radioactive waste continue to build up and poison our planet. This waste needs to be removed and governments will pay well for someone to take it away. Your creation now enables us to safely dispose of this waste, harmlessly removing it from our world. After all, IES works to create a cleaner planet, together we can help achieve this."

"Moving our problem elsewhere is not the answer. What you are suggesting is a form of space landfill. You have no idea what damage this could cause."

"But it is millions of miles away, who is to care as long as we remove it from the Earth. We both get what we want. I would also like to point out the reason that we have so many customers. It's quite ironic that IES are the reason. Do you have any idea how many lives and companies IES have destroyed by forcing their environmental legislation on governments? Increasing waste disposal costs by five thousand times what they once were and imposing millions of dollars of fines for breaches whilst the countries that have abandoned IES continue to pollute with impunity but without the extra cost. How did you think companies in IES controlled countries could ever compete? You didn't because you didn't even consider it. Not a care for the consequences, the people's jobs and livelihoods lost due to the ivory tower preaching of IES. Jim there are many people that despise IES and would gladly see the organisation shut down. I find it quite ironic that we are using IES technology to fix the problem."

"Things have to change, there is no other way. How exactly did you manage to build a CRESI? No one outside my team knows the details and they would never disclose them."

As Jim said this a man appeared from behind a large control panel.

"Hello Jim."

"Brandon! You. But why?"

"Why? How many years have we worked on this project? Every time we fail. We never get any nearer, but you keep going, never admitting that it will just never work. Here is the answer, it makes sense."

"You know why we cannot do this Brandon?"

"Oh, the journal of Marie Duvoux. The three trials. Man and ape like creatures living on a perfect world where technology and nature go hand in hand. Celestial beings visiting to destroy us if we dare break any of the IES golden rules. Fairy tales Jim, just IES fairy tales to keep us all in check."

"You don't really believe that?"

"Do you know how much I could be earning now with my skills in the private sector. But I can't because I'm trapped here in IES, forbidden to work anywhere else in this field. Spied on when you leave. So, your answer as to why. Simple. Money."

"You are a disgrace. I will not help you pollute other worlds and possibly destroy ours."

Brandon walked up to Jim.

"Don't be a fool Jim. Don't mess with these people."

Jim landed his right fist on Brandon's jaw and he fell to the floor. Melanie turned to Jim.

"Nice right hook."

220

Brandon stood up rubbed his jaw and walked over to where Kal was standing.

"You will give me the codes Jim. You have no choice."

"I am sorry that you feel the way you do Jim. I was hoping you would be more co-operative; it would have been so much easier for everyone. But I am afraid contracts have been signed and we have orders to process so I ask you one more time. The codes please."

"No!"

The atmosphere was tense, both Melanie and Jim knew that their lives were now at risk. Jim wondered what they would try next, but he could not give up the codes as the consequences would be unimaginable.

Kal then pointed to a large flat screen television on the wall. It was showing real time footage of three locations. "Jim, on the screen above there are live feeds of three of our operatives, two are at busy Central London railway stations. The briefcases that they are carrying contain high explosives and will be placed in areas that will cause maximum deaths and injury. You can see that one operative is outside a day care centre. I will instruct the operatives to conceal those cases and detonate them unless you co-operate. Now for the very last time. What are the codes!"

"Jim he will do it. Please."

Jim looked at Melanie her face full of concern. What could he do? He couldn't watch innocent people being blown apart?

"Okay. Okay. You are a complete bastard and one day you will pay for this."

Jim relayed the codes to Brandon who immediately walked over to the CRESI control panel. Jim watched as Brandon activated CRESI, the book had already been positioned and CRESI had already laser carved the symbols into the large stone floor. He noticed how they had enlarged the containment field area to cater for the containers of waste products. The crane, which was fully automated, began to move the containers into the field area, onto the large symbol-carved stone. Jim turned to Melanie and took her hand.

"God help us all."

Melanie and Jim were led back to lift and into the upstairs room and ordered to sit and wait for Kal to arrive. They could see the containers being loaded onto the stone as groups of them were phased away to some distant part of space. It was like a conveyor belt with the crane loading more and more containers, leading to more and more waste being dumped.

"There must be a very strong Ley line running under here. I have an awful feeling about this Melanie."

"I only hope that they are true to their word and release us. I just want to get back home away from here."

"I hope I'm wrong, but I think being trapped here will be the least of our worries".

Chapter 35

Daniel had arranged for Carla to be driven straight home once they arrived back in London as she was anxious to see her grandmother. He promised to call if he had any news about Melanie and then made his way back to his own house. Esther called Daniel later that evening and told him that she would collect him in the morning and that she would drive them to the briefing which was taking place at Northwood.

"Good morning Daniel, how are you?"

"All good considering. Carla is back with her grandmother."

"You like her, don't you?"

Daniel hesitated with his reply, feeling slightly embarrassed by Esther's question.

"I think Carla is a genuine person. I think she really cares about people."

"You know that's not what I mean. Anyway, listen to this, I spoke with Aidan earlier and The Reform Team are in place and ready."

"Are we doing the right thing sending them in? They are not soldiers."

"I know, I'm not exactly crazy about it myself, but I have made sure that they have full cover, they are there to break that wall and then get out. Nothing else."

"Okay, but as soon as we retrieve the book, I need to get back to Eden 7."

"Of course. Aidan told me that they have given themselves code names because they thought they sounded cool. He told me what they were, and I agree."

"People criticise IES, yet when I look at what we have done with The Reformers and other programmes like this I just know that it is all worth it."

Daniel and Esther arrived at Northwood RAF Base at 9.00 am, early for the 10.00 am Operation Firestrike briefing. Esther bought them both a coffee and they were escorted to the briefing room. Major Patrick Harding, a veteran soldier of eighteen years, was already present, he had been appointed Gold Firestrike for the duration of the operation.

Esther and Daniel took their seats.

"Ladies and gentlemen, I will outline the overall strategy for Operation Firestrike. Sergeant Johnson will be communications officer for the special operations team, codename Viper, and Sergeant Harris will be the liaison officer for the IES team, codename Guardians. By the way, who chose Guardians?"

Sergeant Harris glanced at Esther and then turned to the Major.

"The IES team chose it themselves. They have also given themselves codenames."

"I see. Anyway, moving on we also have Sergeant Hill who will be the drone operator giving us real-time video of the operation. The operation must be swift. Viper are already in position concealed and awaiting Guardians are currently en route to the area. Their role is to remove the stone wall. Viper reported seeing the iron gates, which covered the underwater entrance, raise and observing a large underwater vessel enter the cave earlier in the morning. This we believe is the submarine containing Jim, Melanie and the book. Viper report that there appears to be little if any security around the area and its position is extremely remote, so we do not anticipate much resistance. It would appear this is being used as a storage area and that they do not consider that it requires any extra protection. Once we give the go ahead, Guardians will move in, remove the wall, and then leave. Viper will enter the structure and overcome any resistance, obtain the book and the hostages and then also leave. They have already concealed a reinforced inflatable boat which they will use to return to a ship which will be anchored offshore.

Any questions? No, Good. Sergeants Harris and Johnson complete your audio and visual checks with your teams. Sergeant Hill check that your drone is good to go. Operation Firestrike will commence thirty minutes from now."

Esther's mobile phone began to ring, it was Kevin. Esther made her excuses and walked into the corridor with Daniel to take the call.

"Hello Kevin."

"Esther, we have just received reports of activity in Eden 7. I will send you the CCTV video that we are receiving straight away."

Kevin streamed the video directly to Esther's mobile. CCTV cameras focused on the ridge area and showed bright lights emanating from the cave. Then, out walked three Shey Atar, Forcarbon, Forfire and Forair. They appeared to be in a heated discussion, almost arguing. Forcarbon then walked away from the other two, looked up towards the sky and opened her mouth. Bellows of red mist began to appear, very quickly covering the entire Eden and the Rangers shed. Visual was lost for a few seconds because of the red mist but then it began to clear. Forair was creating a strong wind which was blowing the mist up into the atmosphere, a large pillar of red mist continued to come from Forcarbon.

"Kevin is this live CCTV?"

"Yes."

"Get in contact with the Rangers at Eden 7 and get them out of there. And see if we can analyse what this red stuff is."

"I will send a pilot to pick them up and arrange for a drone to fly through the mist to collect a sample."

"Good. I wonder what the hell they are doing, and I hope it's not what I suspect."

Esther and Daniel watched the video being streamed to them.

"Esther can you see this? It looks like its stopping; the red mist is stopping."

Esther watched as the mist stopped. All three Shey Atar walked towards the cave, Forcarbon briefly glanced at the camera before returning and following the other two into the cave. In a flash of light they were gone. Daniel looked up from the phone at Esther.

"The book must have been used; they must have done something terrible. It's begun, I have to get that book back to Forcarbon and try and persuade her to undo this."

"Do you know what that mist is?"

"I think so. On my world there are stories of great red clouds covering entire worlds and cleansing away all the poisons. You are the poison."

Esther and Daniel returned to the operations room.

"Sir. Drone deployed and we have visuals."

Esther and Daniel sat at the back of the operations room observing the monitor screens. They could see the face of the cliff and the large stone door.

"Alpha from Zero. Are you ready to go? Over."

"Zero from Alpha. Confirmed we are ready to go. Over."

"Alpha from Zero. All received stand by for go."

"Sir, Guardians confirm ready to go."

***

HMS Manchester was the latest ship in the Royal Navy and was a magnificent vessel and positioned off the coast of Cyprus, Aidan was standing on the deck with his team.

"OK guys don't forget you go in low, head up the cliff face and take the door out. Then you return. Leave the rest to the soldiers. Understood?"

The team all nodded in confirmation.

"Alpha from Zero. Go! Go! Go!"

"Zero from Alpha. All received."

"This is it guys. Good luck! See you all back here soon."

"Energy fields active."

The team each touched one of the symbols on their left arm and a protective field of energy surrounded them.

"Let's go."

They launched from the side of the ship flying across the ocean towards the shore staying about two meters above the surface.

"Viper from Zero."

"Go ahead Zero."

"Guardians are go. ETA ten minutes."

"All received Zero. We are ready to go."

"Thank you Viper. Zero out."

Although the Viper team had been briefed on the operation, they still could not believe what they were watching as the Guardians flew in from the ocean and up the cliff face flying right over them. The Viper team thought it particularly amusing as two of the Guardians gave them a salute as they flew by. At the front of the rock door they positioned themselves and raised their arms, pointing at the door. On their wrists were the blasters developed by IES physicists. They operated like a particle accelerator but on a much smaller scale. Particles travelling at great speed were discharged, they then passed through an ion field. This created an energy pulse which blasted the rock. All appeared to be going to plan, in theory it would only take them about twenty minutes to clear the rock.

***

Inside the compound Kaya was approached by one of her team. She was in the upstairs office on the opposite side of the room to Jim and Melanie.

"We are under attack. They are attempting to blast the door."

Kaya looked at him displaying no emotion.

"Use the gun."

The Guardians were making good progress and were being observed by an impressed Viper team. In the operations room the deployment was being broadcast live on the video screens via the drone and everyone was happy with the progress of the operation. What nobody saw was from high above the door a concealed gun turret began to slowly turn towards the Guardians.

In the operations room Esther's phone bleeped and she looked at the screen which displayed a message from Kevin. 'Urgent. Please call'.

"Hello Kevin, what's the problem?"

"Esther, I have just received news about the Rangers from Eden 7. When the pilot returned, they were all suffering from an unidentified sickness and were transferred and isolated in our medical centre. Esther, the pilot is in a critical condition, but all the other Rangers are dead."

"Oh my God! Then it has begun. I think we may be too late."

"Esther they are analysing samples and I will call you as soon as I hear any more."

"Thank you, Kevin."

Esther ended the call and returned to the operations room. As she took her seat Daniel noticed she had a sad look on her face.

"Esther. What's wrong?"

"Daniel. The Rangers from Eden 7 are all dead."

Daniel looked intently at Esther. There was no doubt now, he thought. It's started and this is probably all my fault.

"Esther if I can get the book back to Forcarbon we may still be able to stop this."

Hailstorm was at the edge of the group when in her peripheral vision she saw a blast of light and then heard a cry. Turning she saw Razor hurling down into the sea.

"Down! Down! Everybody down now!" shouted Alpha.

The Guardians flew down to the surface taking cover behind some rocks. Alpha flew down to the sea, picked up Razor and took him back to where the others were.

"Mikey. You okay?"

Mikey looked at Alpha a little dazed.

"I told you my codename is Razor. Yeah, I'm fine just a little winded. What the hell was that?"

Hailstorm pointed up at the rock face.

"I saw a flash of light. Look up there, a gun."

In the operations room they had observed the blast from the gun.

"Esther this is your call. Do we proceed or abort?"

"We have no choice now. We must get that book."

"Then we have to take that gun out. Tell the Guardians to keep cover and send in the Viper team to neutralise the threat."

"Yes Sir. Alpha receiving? Zero."

"I guess you guys saw that gun. What do we do?"

"Alpha from Zero. Keep cover we will send in the Viper team to take out the weapon."

229

"Zero from Alpha. The gun is too well protected in that rock face. The Viper team will never be able to get to it."

"Alpha from Zero. You have your orders. Keep cover."

Alpha looked at the others who were looking at him. They had heard what Zero had said and were awaiting instructions.

"Anyone want to go back now then that is fine, but I think we can still get that door down."

They all looked and nodded in agreement. They would stay.

"Mikey get yourself back to the ship, you are hurt. I can take the blasts from that gun and give you guys time to take that door down."

"Are you sure Alpha, that gun has quite a kick. And by the way I'm going nowhere."

"Mikey. Sorry Razor if you are sure?"

"I'm staying."

"Okay. I can do it; I can draw the guns fire. Just get that door down as soon as you can."

Alpha looked over to the Viper team. They had obviously been in contact with Zero and were preparing to move out.

"Ready? Let's go."

Alpha flew up first positioning himself in the line of fire of the gun. The others followed and began blasting at the door.

"Alpha from Zero. You are to return to cover immediately. Alpha did you receive? Return to cover immediately."

Alpha ignored the radio. Then it hit him, the first blast. It pushed him back a bit, but his shield was holding. Fortunately, the gun was not rapid fire, requiring at least fifteen seconds to reload. Alpha attempted blasting the weapon, but its metal protective covering was too effective, the blasts just bounced off.

Inside the compound Kaya's mobile began to ring. The display showed EHO.

"Hello."

"Hello Kaya. This is Charlotte, secretary number 3 at Head Office. The operation currently underway has not been authorised by Head Office and has jeopardised principles 1 and 2. You are to return the stolen property to the hostages and release them unharmed immediately. You and your team are then to board Dragonfly and move to Base Two. The Bulgarian and Mr Stone will not be joining you. Please advise The Bulgarian that his employment has been terminated. You have twenty minutes to leave the area before Head Office arrange its sterilisation. Do you understand?"

"Yes."

"Thank you and enjoy the rest of your day. Goodbye."

Kaya walked over to where Jim and Melanie were sitting.

"You are to be released. Go with Dimitrov, he will take you back to Dragonfly. I will bring the book to you."

Jim and Melanie followed Dimitrov, one of Kaya's team, back down to Dragonfly. Kaya walked out of the office and downstairs to where Kal was standing with Brandon.

"What is that noise?"

"Your location has been discovered and they are attempting to gain entry."

Kaya walked over to the book and picked it up from its holder.

"What are you doing?"

"I have been instructed by Head Office to return the book to the hostages, board Dragonfly, and move to Base Two. You are to remain here with Brandon. Head office have terminated your employment. You should have told me this was not authorised."

"If I had told you then you wouldn't have helped me."

Kaya and Kal both knew what remaining in the compound would mean. He was to be eliminated along with his project.

"I'm sorry Kal."

Kaya called one of her team over and told him to get everybody back to Dragonfly. Kal walked back upstairs towards the office with Kaya. Brandon noticed that everyone was leaving.

"Where are you going? You can't leave me here; I still haven't been paid."

Brandon ran across the stone slab towards a set of stairs leading up to where Kal was standing. As he reached the top step, he called to them again.

"Wait for me. You can't leave me here. We had a deal."

As he shouted, one of Kaya's men approached him.

"You stay here."

He pushed Brandon, who fell down the stairs rolling across the stone and hitting his head on the side of one of the containers. He was stunned and as he began to get up from the floor he heard CCRESI.

"Phase shield initiated."

Realising that he was on the stone and CCRESI had begun the process he ran to escape but the shield was already activated, and he was trapped inside.

"Help me! Help me! Somebody please get me out!"

Then he heard CCRESI again.

"Phase shift in 5,4"

"Help me! No please! Somebody please!"

"3,2,1. Phase shift complete."

There was silence and the stone slab was now empty. Somewhere in distant space, floating among waste containers was the lifeless frozen body of Brandon Stone.

Kal sat at his desk staring into space, he knew that he did not have much time. Everyone else was onboard Dragonfly and all that he could hear were the sounds of the crane loading containers and the blasting at the stone door. He previously imagined that he would impress Head Office when he announced the success of his project. Instead it was going to cost him his life. He took a photograph of his family out of his pocket, held it and waited for the inevitable.

Back in the operations room Esther's phone beeped again. Expecting it to be Kevin with an update she looked at the screen. There was no number displayed just a single word. Important. Esther opened and read the text message.

"Hello Esther. This is Georgina, secretary number 7 at Head Office. We have seen the CCTV images at your Eden 7 and must apologise for any inconvenience an unauthorised project may have caused. Your colleagues together with their property are to be released immediately. The person responsible will be dealt with most severely and the project eliminated. You have twenty minutes to remove your staff from the area before sterilisation commences. Once again apologies for any inconvenience and I hope you enjoy the rest of your day."

Before Esther could relay her text message the Viper team called in.

"Zero receiving? Viper."

"Go ahead Viper."

"I don't know if you are getting this, but the gun stopped firing about five minutes ago and the underwater gates have opened. Wait. Wait. A vessel is leaving, it looks like the submarine."

"Viper from Zero. Message received we are repositioning the drone now - standby."

The drone now showed the dark object leaving the enclosure. They watched as the submarine began to surface and then to their surprise it became airborne.

"Viper to Zero. This thing can fly. Can you see this?"

"Viper, yes we are getting this."

"Alpha from Zero. You are to stand down your attack. Stand down your attack."

Alpha and the others had seen the flying submarine and now withdrew down to the ground not far from the Viper team.

Dragonfly silently rose from the sea and flew slowly to the top of the cliff where it landed on a flat area. The drone was now observing Dragonfly and it showed a door on the side of the vessel open and two people walk out. The door closed and Dragonfly silently lifted off, heading horizontally it moved at incredible speed until it could no longer be seen.

Kaya sat alone in the rest area staring into space through the window. They were on their way to Base Two on the dark side of the moon. Kaya had already been advised of her new project; she was to protect The Australian who was the director for the new project involving off Terra Mining. Her mind drifted, briefly thinking about Kal. She had known him for many years, and she was going to miss him. She stood up and made her way to her quarters, after all the recent events she needed to get some rest before she arrived.

Staring at her screen, Esther squinted, looking at the two people standing on the cliff top.

"That's Jim and Melanie. Listen I just received a text, we have about fifteen minutes to get everybody out of there. Get them all out now."

"How do we get them down from that cliff top?" asked Daniel.

"Easy, we use the Guardians."

"Alpha receiving? Zero."

"Go ahead."

"You have less than fifteen minutes to leave the area. Two of you collect the hostages and then all of you return to the ship."

"Understood."

"Hailstorm come with me we will carry the two hostages back. The rest of you make your way straight back to the ship."

Alpha noticed that the Viper team were already in their boat as he and Hailstorm flew up to the top of the cliff. They landed by the surprised looking Melanie.

"You guys can fly?"

"No time for chit chat Ma'am we need to leave now. Hold on tight we are going for a ride," replied Hailstorm.

Both took off with their respective passengers holding on tightly as they headed out across the ocean, Alpha carried the book. They landed safely on HMS Manchester where Aidan and the rest of the team were waiting.

"Well done guys, good job."

"We still didn't manage to break through the door," replied Razor in a disappointed voice.

"I think someone is about to do that for us."

They looked towards the distant coastline and saw the missiles approaching. The explosion was massive, there would be nothing left of the compound. No evidence that it had ever existed. Later that day Syrian television broadcast a report of an explosion at one of its factories and that there were no injuries.

Chapter 36

Esther thanked the Major and his team for their excellent work and left the building with Daniel. On the way back to the car she telephoned Aidan.

"Aidan how are your team? Are they all okay?"

"They are all fine. Mikey was a little winded but he's very resilient."

"Well, please tell them that I am very proud of them."

"I will. To be honest they really enjoyed it. The twins said it makes a change from landscaping."

"Jim and Melanie, are they okay too?"

"They are both fine. They had their mobile phones returned but I have asked them not to make any calls until we get back to London. The military are arranging flights for all of us."

"Good. Tell them I will meet them when they arrive and explain everything."

"Will do."

"What is happening about the book."

"That is all in hand, transport to Eden 7 is being arranged where it will be handed over to Daniel as agreed."

"Good. Well done."

"Esther is it true what I have heard about the Rangers at Eden 7?"

"I am afraid it is Aidan, but I can't really discuss it now. I will explain everything when you get back."

"Okay. Goodbye Esther."

"Goodbye."

Esther and Daniel drove back to IES Headquarters in London where transport to Eden 7 had already been organised for Daniel.

"Daniel are you sure that you do not want me to accompany you?"

"No Esther. We have no clue as to what caused the deaths of the Rangers yet and the Eden could still be dangerous. Besides, you need to co-ordinate what action we may need to take when we establish the cause of death."

"You honestly believe that we have any course of action to take? I am not so sure."

"If you don't mind, I would like to see Carla before I leave. Just in case I don't come back."

"Just in case you don't come back. Would they really harm you?"

"Maybe one would."

Once they arrived at IES Daniel did not go inside but unlocked his car which was parked in the car park. As he did so Esther wished him good luck. He smiled and set off on what may be his last drive to Carla's flat. Esther headed to her office, where she had some important calls to make.

Daniel called Carla and told her that he was on his way over, as he turned the corner, he could see her by the kerbside waiting for him.

"Daniel is everything okay? You sounded a bit worried when you called."

"Everything is fine I just wanted to visit you before I leave. I need to go back to Eden 7 to return the book. How is Betty?"

"Oh, she's fine. In fact, she has gone to a tea dance."

"Glad she's feeling better."

"She has so much life in her now. You know she has a boyfriend. Her dance partner Mr Kipatalos. She calls him her toy boy."

Daniel laughed.

"Thank you so much for what you did for her. It is so strange suddenly, I feel as if she doesn't need me looking after her anymore. It's a bit sad when your grandmother has a better social life than you do."

Carla looked at Daniel, she could see the concern on his face.

"Let me go with you."

"No. No you can't."

"Why not?"

"It is just best if I go alone."

"You are keeping something back from me. Something is wrong isn't it?"

Daniel took Carla's hand.

"Please just trust me. It is safer if you stay here. I will come back as soon as I possibly can."

Carla looked deep into his eyes, she could tell that he was worried, and now she was too.

"Please be careful."

"I will."

Daniel winked and walked back towards his car.

"Daniel!"

Daniel spun round as Carla ran up to him. Carla hugged him and then kissed him. Daniel held her tightly, he wished he could hold her forever but knew that he had to go. He looked at her, smiled, got back into his car and drove off into the distance.

Esther was sitting at her desk sipping her coffee. She was expecting an update on the cause of death of the Rangers and she was dreading what she might hear. Suddenly the phone rang, it was her secretary.

"Good morning Esther, I have a call from the Minister for you."

"Thank you. Put him through,"

"Esther, what's the latest."

"We have the book and it is on its way with Daniel to Eden 7. We have the Eden under surveillance, nothing has happened since the mist incident.

"Have we any information on the cause of death yet?"

"I am expecting a call imminently I and will let you know as soon as I hear."

"Okay. The PM is hosting a video conference call later today so please obtain as much detail as possible. We need to know what we are dealing with. I will speak with you later."

"Goodbye Sir."

Esther looked out of her window into the busy street below, everything was just carrying on as if nothing had happened. She wondered how it would all look maybe a month from now. The thought of every person in the world dying, leaving not a living soul was just too much to comprehend. She needed to get out for some fresh air and decided to go to the Exhibition Centre. Esther telephoned ahead, Kevin was already there as were Sonia and Oliver. Esther parked her car and went straight to the control room where Kevin was waiting.

"Hello Esther."

"Hello Kevin, I see it's still very busy."

"Yes, you just missed Sonia, she popped out for a break. Sonia and Oliver are loving the crowds, they are far larger and better than anyone could have imagined. The interest around the environmental issues is just incredible. You should be proud of what's being achieved here."

"I am proud of everyone. I just hope it's not all been for nothing."

"Still no update concerning the Rangers?"

"No, not yet. I will give them another hour and then chase them up. Any news from Aidan?"

"Yes, he called in. He and the team are on their way back but will not be here for several hours yet."

Esther's mobile phone rang. It was Julianna, the IES Senior Medical Director.

"Hello Julianna"

"Esther, I have some news for you, and I'm afraid it is not good."

"I suspected as much. Go on."

Despite our best efforts the pilot has also died. They were all exposed to a virus. This particular strain is one that I have never seen before, it specifically targets the human genome. The reason they died so quickly was because of the high level of concentrated exposure.

After analysis we have established that lower levels of infection will still be fatal, but over a longer period."

"How long?"

"After initial exposure, the virus will incubate for four to five days. Then the subject will experience a slight fever for one or two days before the virus blocks the electrical signals to the heart resulting in cardiac arrest. It is very quick."

"As I feared. Is there any treatment or vaccine?"

"If I had more time perhaps, but I'm afraid at this moment the chances of finding any kind of cure or treatment are zero."

"I see."

"Esther I'm afraid it gets worse. The virus is airborne, and it is everywhere. The whole world is infected. I'm sorry Esther."

"Thank you, Julianna. Please keep this to yourself. I will be in touch. Goodbye."

"Was that the update you were waiting for? Do we know what it is?"

"I'm sorry Kevin, I can't explain now. I will speak to you all later. Would you mind leaving the office as I have a call to make."

"Of course, I will go and find Sonia."

Kevin left the office and Esther called the Minister. Esther explained to him what she had been told. As a result, she was directed to keep the news classified. They both agreed that Daniel was the only hope now.

Kevin and Sonia then joined Esther in the control room. She looked around at all the families, they were enjoying the exhibits totally oblivious to the terrible disease that they were all infected with. She had never considered herself to be a religious person but now found herself thinking. "Dear God, please don't let this happen." Some hours later the Centre was winding down in preparation to close and the last of the visitors were leaving. Esther's mobile rang again, it was Daniel.

"Esther the book is here. I am going to call them now. I have no idea when or if they will reply but I will let you know when I have more news."

"Daniel you have to convince them to stop this. We know what it is, and the world has about seven days before everyone dies."

"I understand."

Once the Centre was closed Esther instructed everyone to go home and get some rest and that she would arrange a team meeting for the following day.

The following morning the Minister called Esther. He ordered her to say nothing to anyone, not even her team. Her protests were dismissed, and she was told that the subject was not up for debate, she had no choice. The Minister advised that a meeting of world leaders had taken place. The decision had been made that the public were not to be made aware of anything at this stage, and that information would be released soon. The plan was to encourage people to be at home on the final days of the infection, so that they could be with their families in their final days. In the meantime, a delegation would be arranged to try and meet with the Shey Atar if Daniel was unsuccessful, but they also realised that they had little hope of success.

Esther met with her team as promised and explained that the investigation was still ongoing and there was no update as to the cause of the Rangers deaths yet. She hated having to lie but realised that it was for the best.

In the meantime, at Eden 7, Daniel was sitting on the ridge waiting for a response. He looked out over the Eden, fondly recalling the last time he was there and how much he enjoyed spending time with Carla. He knew that he had been waiting for over twenty four hours and had still heard nothing. He picked up his mobile and called Carla.

"Hello Carla. How are you?"

"Hello Daniel, I'm fine. Just sitting at home with Betty."

"Oh, she's at home for a change then?"

"Yes. Girls night in. How are you? Any news?"

"Nothing yet. I hope to hear something soon, I have been waiting for over a day." As he said that a flash of light caught Daniels eye. "Carla, I have to go. I will call you back soon."

Daniel ended the call before Carla could answer. As he turned around, he saw Forcarbon walk out of the cave.

"Forcarbon I have returned the book."

"I am sorry it is too late Daniel. They have caused much harm and they will cause future harm to other worlds. It cannot be allowed to happen."

"But it was only a few greedy people who caused the damage. They have been stopped and punished. And it was my fault the book was taken. Please you cannot punish the whole world for the mistakes of so few."

Forcarbon took the book from Daniel and began to walk back towards the cave.

"Please Forcarbon. If someone must be punished, then punish me. I will give my life it that is what is required."

"You would sacrifice yourself for them? Why?"

"I have lived among them for so long. I see the good in them. They have changed so much."

Forcarbon looked quizzically at Daniel as she considered what he had said.

"The book will be removed and never will they use symbols again. I will give them another chance. But this will be their last be sure that you tell them."

Inside the cave further flashes of light appeared, Forfire and Forair emerged from the darkness. Forcarbon turned to Forfire.

"I have the book; Daniel has explained what happened. I am prepared to give them one last chance."

"No. No more. This will end here!"

Forcarbon walked over to where Forfire was standing. Forcarbon placed her hand on Forfire's face of grey cracked skin with red heat below it. Any mortal touching her would have been incinerated.

"Search your soul my sister. Do you really feel that this is the will of Atar? I do not."

Forfire took Forcarbon's hand and pulled it away from her face.

"This will not be undone."

"I am sorry my sister, but it will be undone. That is my decision to make."

Forcarbon walked away and looked up to the sky. She opened her mouth but before she could do anything, she was blown back against the rock face. Forair focused a blast of air that held her to the rock. Forfire raised her hands and a jet of heat blasted the rock above Forcarbon. Daniel ran towards them, the heat burning his skin.

"No! Let her go!"

Forair turned to him and a blast of wind blew him down off of the ridge. Daniel, hurt and bruised could only watch. He was powerless to help.

The rock became molten and slid slowly downward towards Forcarbon. As it reached her, she changed in appearance, she became transparent, she had literally become a diamond. Slowly the molten rock continued until Forcarbon was completely covered. The rock cooled and she was gone, entombed in the rock. Daniel realised that she was his only hope and now she was gone. Forfire called down to Daniel.

"Instruct the Ambassadors that they are to return. They will be collected tomorrow. You too will return."

"I will stay."

"As you wish. We will bear witness to this cleansing. Now go."

**

Esther had been alerted to the activity on the Eden CCTV and had witnessed the events as they unfolded. She knew that Daniel had failed in his mission. All hope was gone. She called the Minister with an update. He, in turn advised her that all future decisions would be taken at senior government level. She would not be included in any further event planning, and that she would follow instructions as they were released to the public. Daniel returned and joined Esther at the Exhibition Centre. He advised all the IES Ambassadors that they were being recalled and that they would be collected the following day. Esther and Daniel sat at a table in the restaurant area.

"Esther I am so sorry. I wish that there were something I could do."

"You tried your best. This all feels so unreal. Just thinking that seven days from now everyone will be dead."

"Have you told any of the others?"

"No. I have been specifically instructed not to. But should I? I don't know. How will knowing help? Where are you going to go for the final days?"

"I am going to Carla's. I would like to be with her."

"Are you going to tell her?"

"No. I am not going to tell her. What about you? Where will you go?"

"I think I may just stay here. There is no one at home for me, and I have no family. I am not afraid of death Daniel. I just wonder what it was all for? What was the point of it all? I suppose it was our arrogance thinking that we were the superior life in the universe. Thinking that we answer to no one. By the way I heard that the government delegation didn't get very far. The large balls of fire that were thrown at them put an end to their bid."

A television news feed was constantly transmitting on a large screen on the far wall and their conversation was interrupted when they heard the announcement.

"We have some breaking news coming in. Meteorologists are advising of a rare solar event involving flares that will occur five days from now. They are advising that everyone should remain in their homes for two days. There is no risk of any harm but as a precaution people are being advised to stay at indoors.

Governments are arranging temporary shelters for homeless people. Power networks will be shut down to avoid any damage and all flights will be grounded. We will bring you further updates on this story as we get them."

"Well that's the cover story then. Daniel I'm going to go home I will see you tomorrow."

"Goodnight Esther."

After Esther had left Daniel called Carla and asked if she fancied dinner somewhere. She eagerly agreed and asked if they could go to La Serra.

A short time later Daniel pulled up outside Carla's flat. She was ready and waiting for him in the foyer. "Daniel, I saw the news report. What is happening?"

Daniel thought carefully before answering. He knew that he could not tell her a lie, she would know. He had to tell her the truth. He pulled the car over and explained what had happened. Carla sat staring ahead silently. She turned to him, a tear flowing down her face.

"I'm so sorry Carla." Daniel leaned over and held her. Carla hugged him back.

"I can't believe it. Is there nothing that can be done?"

"Sorry. Forcarbon is gone and the others will not change their minds. Carla come with me to my world, maybe I can get them to save you?"

"No. I'm staying with Betty."

"I want to stay with you. May I?"

"Of course, I was hoping you would. Daniel please take me home now; we can skip dinner."

Chapter 37

The days ticked by and Esther continued in her usual professional style, behaving as if nothing was wrong. She attended the Exhibition Centre every day and enjoyed seeing the visitors having fun and interacting with her team. She found it difficult not being able to tell them the truth, they had all seen the news reports and questioned her, but she said that it was pure coincidence and not to worry.

Preparations were being made to close the Centre for the two days when Daniel arrived. The two of them strolled around idly chatting.

"I've come to say goodbye Esther."

"I thought you would. How are things at Carla's?"

"Fine. Betty thinks it been her birthday for the last few days. Carla has been spoiling her with all sorts of things."

"You told her, didn't you?"

"I had to."

Daniel gave Esther her hug. Esther looked at him and kissed him on the cheek.

"Goodbye Daniel."

Esther sat alone in the control room surveying the empty Exhibition Centre. Everyone had now left, and most people were at home following the government advice. Suddenly the door opened and in walked Kevin. He was holding a bottle of brandy and two glasses.

"Drink?"

"Why aren't you at home? The solar flare arrives soon."

"Do you honestly believe that I would fall for that crap?"

"No. I didn't think you would."

"I saw you with Daniel. I guessed you were saying goodbye. Is he leaving with the others?"

"No, he wants to stay. He has decided to be with Carla."

Kevin poured them both a large drink.

"There's plenty more where that came from. Cheers."

"Kevin do you have no one you would like to be with? Family?"

"This is my family."

Esther walked to the window and looked outside."

"It is so quiet. No people, No vehicles. Everyone is inside it's so surreal."

"Esther are you afraid?"

"Kevin, I have faced death many times in my lifetime. Death does not worry me. What scares me is the thought of dying alone. That is my biggest fear. The thought of having no one with me in my last minutes."

"You won't be alone Esther. I will be here with you."

Esther walked over to Kevin and placed her hand on his shoulder and smiled.

"What about you Kevin are you afraid?"

"Not afraid, terrified. I cannot bear this waiting. I just wish it were all over. But also irritated and angry. You see no matter how hard I try to make some logical sense of this I can't. It makes no sense at all."

"Kevin, life sometimes has a way of making no sense."

"You know what else I think about?"

"What?"

"Aidan."

"I think about the others too."

"No, I mean his situation. Not just Aidan but everyone else who knows what's about to happen and has a family or loved ones around them."

"You think that Aidan knows?"

"Esther. He's not stupid, of course he knows. He gave me a hug before he left. He has never given me a hug before. He asked me to give you this. He said he couldn't give it to you himself."

Kevin took a small book from his pocket. It was titled 'For Your Darkest Days' by Celia Thrupshaw. He handed it to Esther.

Esther took the book, as she looked at it, she smiled.

"I had no idea Aidan was interested in poetry.

"This is something that I gave to him many years ago when he was going through a bad patch. Bless him."

"How do you deal with that Esther? That is what I think about. How do you sit down with your family around you knowing they are going to die and not be able to do anything about it? It is beyond terrible. The whole thing is driving me crazy; I just wish it was over, I hate just waiting for the inevitable."

Esther could see the distress in her friend's face. She respected and admired him, to Esther he was like family.

"I will get us another drink."

Esther picked up her bag walked over to the side table where the bottle was sitting. Kevin sat in the chair his back to her. She opened her handbag and looked at the revolver. Esther picked up the gun, she decided that it would be quick for Kevin, he would not feel a thing, she would end her friend's distress.

Suddenly from the street outside there was a crack that sounded like a lightning bolt. The noise was incredibly loud and the wave of pressure that accompanied it was so strong that Kevin felt it in his chest.

"What the hell was that?" asked Kevin, jumping up from his chair and looking out of the window.

Esther quickly placed the gun back into her handbag.

"I have no idea. Was it a lightning strike?"

"The skies are clear. Maybe an explosion."

Esther's phone rang. It was Aidan.

"Did you hear that?"

"Yes. I thought it was lightning. Sorry Aidan I have to go; I have another incoming call."

Esther looked at her mobile and saw that it was the Minister calling.

"Esther did you hear it?"

"Yes, any idea what it was?"

"No. But we are getting reports that it was heard around the world. It was everywhere. Is there any activity at the Eden?"

Esther looked closely at the monitor.

"Minister they are kneeling. Wait something is happening."

Esther watched the CCTV intently. She could see large black clouds forming, the darkest clouds she had ever seen. Then from the clouds a bolt of lightning struck Forfire throwing her to the ground. A second bolt struck Forair dispersing her form. Then more bolts continually striking the rock face. Strike after strike hit the target until Forcarbon was completely uncovered. Slowly she changed back from diamond to her normal form. She knew what she had to do. She could feel Atar's presence and knew his will.

Forair began to reform her shape, Forfire got back on her knees. Forcarbon looked up to the sky and opened her mouth. Billows of white mist appeared covering the Eden and blocking the CCTV for a few moments before clearing. Forair was forcing the mist up into the atmosphere and around the world. The skies cleared and Forfire and Forair entered the cave. Immediately in a flash of light they were both gone.

Esther told the Minister what she had just witnessed and that she would immediately call Daniel and despatch him to Eden

250

7. The Minister promised her that he would send a scientific team to the Eden to analyse the mist.

"Daniel it's Esther. I take it you heard the noise. You must return to the Eden. Forcarbon is free and she has done something, I am not sure what. I just pray that she has helped us. It is vital that you go and speak to her."

Hours passed and Esther waited for an update from Daniel. She could see him sitting with Forcarbon, it seemed as if they had been speaking for ages. The scientific team had visited the site and left with samples but again she had not received an update. Forcarbon eventually stood up and walked into the cave, following a flash of light she also disappeared. Almost immediately Esther's phone rang.

"Esther. We have been given one last chance. Everything is going to be okay."

"Oh, thank God. I will see you back here."

Esther immediately called the Minister to tell him the news.

"Esther our team have analysed the samples. You are correct, it is an airborne phage that targets the virus. It's a cure."

Worldwide press releases were issued advising that the solar flares trajectory had changed and that it would no longer collide with the Earth. It instructed people to return to their normal routines. Life went on. The entire population of the world were completely unaware of how close they came to being wiped out. The incident strengthened support from Governments around the world for IES which was now welcomed by almost every country.

Chapter 38

The following week DI Burns arranged a meeting in his office between himself, Simon, Melanie and Carla. "Following all of our recent adventures I am taking the three of you out for a drink. I have arranged your duties. Be in La Serra at 2.00 pm next Thursday. I will not accept any excuses for no attendance". The three of them looked at one another in surprise.

"Do you think that wise following the last time that we had a drink on duty guvnor?" asked Simon.

"Don't worry, this has the blessing of our Borough Commander"

Thursday arrived, it was rather a drab afternoon and one by one the four of them met at the restaurant. It was not as busy during the day as it was during the evening and they took their places at a table. Jaz immediately recognised them and made his way straight over. "Good afternoon my friends. Nice to see you again. Drinks?"

"Please may I start a bar tab and put everything on it?" asked DI Burns.

"Of course, my friend."

The quartet ordered their drinks which arrived shortly afterwards. Jaz in the meantime was at the other side of the restaurant cleaning and tidying the bar.

Simon, as usual, was dressed impeccably in a dark fitted suit, and co-ordinated shirt, tie and pocket square. He smelt of sophisticated expensive aftershave.

Everyone else was dressed very casually, DI Burns in a pair of chinos and a shirt, the girls in jeans and blouses.

DI Burns then announced. "I have something to tell you. I just wanted to let you all know before you hear it from anyone else. I have just handed in my resignation?"

"What! No Guv you got to be joking. What are you going to do?" asked Simon, clearly shocked.

"You all know that botanicals are my real passion. I joined the Police because it paid well. Following the exhibition, I have been offered and accepted a position working with Oliver at IES."

"Congratulations." said Carla. "I am so pleased for you."

"Well I guess that just leaves us three then?" said Simon.

Melanie looked at Carla and smiled and then glanced at Simon.

"Not exactly. I was telling Carla before you arrived. I've accepted a job with IES too. Working on a field crew. I start next week, and we are off to Peru. Apparently there have been sightings of some previously undiscovered prehistoric animals."

"Oh great. Well Carla that just leaves us then." said Simon, winking at her.

"I'm afraid not. I have been given a one-year career break. Daniel has asked me to travel to his world and I have said 'yes'. I am not even sure that I will ever return to the Police. I will see how it goes."

"Oh great. You get to hunt dinosaurs. You get to space travel and you Guv get your dream job."

"Simon you love this job and you are a good copper. You will go far. Besides, after what we have been involved in, we will all stay in touch."

The girls nodded in agreement. Simon looked up in the direction of the restaurant entrance.

As he did so a man entered and walked over to the bar. "Hello nice to see you again Dom" said Jaz as they shook hands. The man then walked over to their table. He was six feet tall, late twenties, very handsome in a clean-cut way. Dressed very smartly but very casually. Carla and Melanie looked at one another and Melanie raised one of her eyebrows.

"Okay well good luck to you all in your new ventures. I will still be here in The Met. Sorry but I need to go now my boyfriend is here. We are going shopping."

The man kissed Simon on the cheek.

"Ready Simon?"

Carla, Melanie and DI Burns all looked at one another with a look of amazement. Nobody said anything. Carla's mouth moved but no words came out.

"I would like you to meet Dominic. Carla and Melanie, you have actually met him before but just didn't realise. Do you remember the last time that we were all in here? Dom was hosting the karaoke under his stage name 'Dommy Natricks'. I was bursting to tell you all but wasn't sure how anyone would take it. After what we have been through, I guess it is all neither here nor there really"

They all greeted Dominic and then Carla turned to Simon.

"Simon. You're gay?"

"Yes of course. How could you not tell? I dress immaculately, am smart, look after myself, always have clean nails, always smiling, easy to get on with, I am a stereotypical gay."

Carla looked at Melanie and smiled.

"That is so fantastic. Pleased to meet you Dominic."

Simon got up, he and Dominic left the restaurant with the remaining trio still looking at one another in disbelief. DI Burns explained that he had a lot of odds and ends to tidy up, paid the bill and he too left.

"Of course, I knew he was gay all along," said Melanie.

"You absolutely did not," replied Carla sarcastically.

***

Weeks later Carla was ready to leave on her trip with Daniel. Betty had given her blessing and Carla knew that she would be fine.

Daniel and Carla had said all their goodbyes and headed to Eden 7. As they were about to enter the cave, a helicopter approached. It landed and an elderly lady disembarked. Daniel recognised her immediately and walked over to meet her.

"Marie! Quelle surprise?" *Marie! What a surprise.*

"Daniel. Mon cher ami. Mais veuillez parler en Anglaise." *Daniel. My dear friend. But please speak in English.*

Daniel walked over and hugged her.

"I heard you were leaving and had to say goodbye. Who is this pretty young lady?"

"Marie please meet Carla. Carla this is Marie Duvoux an old friend of mine."

"Pleased to meet you Carla. Will you be travelling with Daniel?"

"Yes, I will."

Marie took Carla's hand.

"Listen to me. Make the most of every minute and be prepared for some excitement. You are about to have some amazing experiences. Let me give you some advice. One day you may visit a settlement on the outskirts of the stones that belong to the Shey Atar who commands time."

"Marie. Il vous est interdit de parler de cela." *Marie. You are forbidden to talk about this.*

"Je ne m'inquiète pas. Elle devrait être prévenue, comme j'aurais dû l'être. À ce jour, ce que j'ai vu me hante encore." *I do not care. She should be warned, as I should have been. To this day what I saw still haunts me.*

Marie turned back to Carla.

255

"There is a symbol there that you will be given the opportunity to use. You will only be able to use it once. It has the power to show you what might have been if a moment in your life, of your choosing, had occurred differently. Carla listen to me carefully. No matter how great your desire. No matter how desperate you are to see what might have been. Please decline the offer. Things do not always turn out as you would hope."

Marie was gripping Carla's hand, her face contorted with emotion. Marie gathered herself and smiled at Carla, releasing her hand she turned to Daniel.

"Good luck Daniel and please give my love to Ezra."

Daniel gave Marie a kiss on the cheek. Marie gave him a hug and stared into his eyes with a smile on her face. Marie then turned and headed back to the waiting helicopter. As they both walked into the cave Carla held Daniels hand. There was a bright light and Forcarbon appeared.

"What did Marie mean?"

"It is nothing. Carla no harm will ever come to you I promise. I will always protect you."

"I know you will."

Daniel leant over and kissed Carla on the lips.

"Carla, there's something I need to do. Will you wait here for me? I will not be long."

"Of course I will."

Daniel walked over to Forcarbon.

"Forcarbon I need to make something right. A man that we did not support in his desperation to save his ill daughter began this. It ultimately cost him his life. Will you see her? She is seriously ill and dying."

Forcarbon glanced at Carla then turned back to Daniel.

"I will see her. Tell me where she is."

"The grandparents may be angry with us and not allow a visit."

"Trust me Daniel, they will."

Daniel explained which hospital Corin was in. He had always been amazed at how the Shey Atar knew everything. It was as if the whole universe was a map in their heads and they could effortlessly travel to a specific location with pinpoint accuracy, no matter how remote.

Forcarbon transported them both to a deserted corridor in Corin's hospital. Both of her grandparents were at her side as she slept. Daniel and Forcarbon approached the grandparents. Daniel had decided he would introduce Forcarbon as Anna, a work colleague of Don.

"My name is Daniel, and this is Anna she used to work with Don and wanted to speak with Corin."

The grandparents agreed, strangely mesmerised by Anna. They watched outside the room through the window and as Anna sat on Corin's bed, Corin woke and sat up. They watched as Anna spoke with Corin who smiled and laughed. Then they saw Anna lean over and whisper in Corin's ear. As Anna moved away, she placed her forefinger over her lips and smiled. Corin placed her right hand over her heart and raised her left hand and was saying something. Corin turned to the empty chair by her bed and held out her arms. Anna stood up, stroked Corin's hair and left the room.

"Thank you for letting me see Corin." said Forcarbon. She and Daniel then quietly walked off down the hospital corridor. Corin's grandparents went back into her ward.

"Will she be okay?" asked Daniel.

"Daniel there are some things that even the Shey Atar cannot change. But don't worry about Corin, she's going home."

Daniel glanced back at Corin's room them turned and followed Forcarbon, from Corin's room her grandparents looked at them as they left.

"What did that lady say sweetheart?"

"She told me a secret and made me promise not to tell."

"Sweety, why were you looking at the empty chair?"

"Silly grandma. I was talking to Daddy. He's come to take me home."

Corin lay down and went to sleep. Her grandparents hugged one another, tears running down their faces.

Forcarbon and Daniel returned to the cave where Carla was waiting.

"Are you both ready?"

Daniel looked at Carla and Carla nodded to him.

"Yes. Yes, we are."

A bright light came from nowhere and then they were both gone.

In the control room Esther watched the CCTV monitor.

"Good luck Daniel. See you soon." Esther said to the screen.

Meanwhile in a remote rural area of Bulgaria. Two men were sitting around a campfire, telling a group of wide eyed disbelieving children of the night they encountered The Beast of Limehouse.

Printed in Poland
by Amazon Fulfillment
Poland Sp. z o.o., Wrocław

93493473R00145